FRESHMAN **YEAR**

FRESHMAN YEAR

Kenneth Winfield Emerton

authorHOUSE®

AuthorHouse™
1663 Liberty Drive
Bloomington, IN 47403
www.authorhouse.com
Phone: 1 (800) 839-8640

Published by AuthorHouse   05/13/2015

ISBN: 978-1-5049-1249-5 (sc)
ISBN: 978-1-5049-1248-8 (e)

Library of Congress Control Number: 2015907735

Print information available on the last page.

I would like to dedicate my first book to my cousin Haley, an amazing young author. Your writing surpasses mine at your age by a mile. You will go far.

Special thanks to the real Mr. and Mrs. Morrison. Mr. Morrison, you were the first person to take my writing seriously. Mrs. Morrison, you were the second. The two of you have influenced me more than I will ever be able to tell you. I truly believe that I am a better writer for taking the advice of both of you. Thank you a million times over!

I would also like to give special thanks to Taylor Swift, whose song "Fifteen" inspired the storyline that eventually became this book.

Part One

SEPTEMBER TO DECEMBER

CHAPTER 1

Carol Robinson was an outcast. She had been this way ever since she was a child. She had never been very interested in the same things as her classmates. She had always been more content being alone and writing than talking to other people, which had always worked for her. She had always figured, why bother with a lot of friends when you could easily be just as entertained by your own thoughts and creations.

She had always enjoyed writing, as long as she could remember. It was one of the only true passions that she had in life. Her favorite part of writing was being able to create her own worlds and live in them, much like in dreams, as if they were the real one. Other children had always bullied her because of this, calling her names like "freak" or "weirdo". She had always felt sorry for them, rather than feeling upset about the fact that she was being bullied. This was because they did not have the talent that she had and so, for the most part, lived in the 'real' world, with the exception of video games and TV shows.

Carol had always been proud of being an outcast, but now, as she walked into Bucksport High School, she felt sick, knowing that high school kids were stereotypically worse than any other breed of person. And since her mother and her had just moved to this town so that her mother could begin a new job, she was worried that she may not make it through her first day alive.

David Craven was also an outcast. His parents had died in a car accident when he was six year old and he had been in and out of foster homes ever since. He had been with his newest foster parent, Brenda, almost a year, and had finished his 8th grade year under her supervision. Brenda was the nicest of any foster parents' he had ever had. Not only did she buy him gifts, she was in general, a good person. She had been very welcoming in bringing David not only into her home, but the town of Bucksport, where David had never been.

He hadn't made any friends because he had only talked to teachers. He enjoyed having intelligent conversations, and teachers were a lot better at that than most of his classmates. He always sat in the back of the classroom and barely passed his classes because he had his mind on other things like his future and what he would do after high school.

When he wasn't thinking about his future, he could always be found writing. He loved to write. He always had. In David's previous foster family, one of his foster brothers had taken a story he had written and torn it to shreds. David had beaten the boy until he had blood coming out of every corner of his face and a bruised rib cage. The family called the foster agency and had him out of their family as fast as they could. David was not a violent person, but the boy had taken the one thing that David had always had just to himself and ruined it. David later rewrote the story because he had thought it had been so well done.

David thought about the incident as he walked into Bucksport High School and wondered how many times in the next four years he would need to fight for his life. This was where the bullies of all bullies roamed free. He hoped as he walked that he could make it through his first day without one mean name, one rude comment, his head in a toilet or one trip down the stairs.

The first day of school was September third, a Thursday. David and Carol both spent the morning exploring the halls, trying to memorize the locations of different classrooms which were on their schedules. When the bell rang, they went to home room as instructed by the principal,

Mrs. Jodi King, who had came on the various intercoms around the school. Unknowingly, David and Carol were both in the same homeroom.

This was the homeroom of Mr. William Morrison. William Morrison was a thirty something year old English teacher who had been teaching at Bucksport High for ten years and he knew the school inside and out.

He had originally planned on going to college for writing, but he had decided that he would continue writing no matter what career he had, so he had changed his major to secondary education with a concentration in English, which was also a career that had always interested him.

After college, he had, like most graduates, taken a few minor teaching jobs, some which were even substitute positions. He had finally heard from his friend Robert that Bucksport High, the high school which they had both attended, had a new position open in the English department.

William Morrison now stood, coffee in hand, in front of the homeroom full of brand new Freshmen, waiting for them to quiet down. He immediately noticed a young girl writing frantically in a notebook. She seemed to be very passionate with it. He watched her for a few minutes before realizing that the room had grown silent. He began speaking to the freshmen.

"Hello, I am Mr. Morrison and I will be your homeroom teacher for the next four years," William began. "If you have any questions any time within those four years, you are always welcome to ask me. I hope to be your good friend and I know that I will have some of you this semester, for I am a Freshmen English teacher."

All of the freshmen just looked at him. He could see they were tired and confused. "So, I will see some of you today in class." William finished as he walked back to his desk, shaking his head as he walked.

The announcements began and the students were instructed to stand for the Pledge of Allegiance. The students did as they were told and stood, and recited the Pledge. All except for Carol, who was deep in her writing and had not even heard the morning announcements begin. This intrigued William and he thought that she had a lot of potential as a writer and hoped that he had her in class.

David stood but did not recite the Pledge of Allegiance. Instead he just stood there, looking over at Carol with a thoughtful look on his face. He was thinking the same thing as William and more. Students were instructed to sit back down and did so. Carol smiled and sat back in her seat, a look of achievement on her face. She closed her notebook and put it in her backpack.

William gave everyone their locker numbers and dismissed them to their classes. They all put their things in their lockers and blindly began wondering around trying to find their classes.

David was lucky, because he didn't have to even leave the room for his first class, which was English with Mr. Morrison.

Carol also had that class first thing, but, blinded with excitement from finishing a story that she had began at the beginning of the summer, she left the room. She snapped out of it and wondered back to Williams' room, where everyone was already sitting down and William was handing out a short introductory assignment.

She went to the back of the room and sat in the only seat left, right next to David. She got the assignment and smiled. It was a short story assignment. She would ace this with flying colors.

Next to her, David was smiling just as much, because he knew that he too would ace this with no problem whatsoever.

William stood up at the front of the class and began explaining the assignment. "People hear the words 'short story', and they panic because they aren't really sure what is expected. A short story can be anywhere between four and forty pages long, or even shorter. For your first assignment, I want you to write a short story. This assignment is really just my way of finding out how you write, so I know where to start with you. The story can be about anything you feel, and it may also be biographical. This is to be passed in tomorrow morning at the beginning of class. With that said, you may begin writing."

While the rest of the class sat in awe at the thought of writing a short story the first thing in the morning, Carol had already taken off like a rocket, writing, smiling and erasing faster than anyone William had ever seen.

Even David sat there, amazed at the speed that she was writing. He was a good writer, but even he couldn't have come up with a story *that* fast. Five minutes later he was off, writing a story about a poor old man who was alone and always got pushed around by society.

At the end of class, Carol was the only one finished. Carol took the story up to Mr. Morrison, who had a look of amazement in his eyes.

"You know you could still work on it tonight, right?" William asked.

"It is exactly as I want it," Carol said. "I am finished with it."

"Alright then, see you tomorrow, uh, Carol right?" Mr. Morrison asked.

"Yes, Carol Robinson," Carol said, extending her hand. William returned the hand shake and she turned and walked towards the door. David stopped her at the door.

"Hi, I'm David Craven," David stammered. "I, uh, also enjoy writing very much. I was wondering if maybe sometime we could go somewhere and just, you know, talk about writing."

"Sure, I'd like that," Carol said, staring down at the ground, suppressing a small smile. "I've got to get to class."

As Carol ran to her next class, David watched her for a moment, took a nervous deep breath and proceeded to his own class.

Period seven was a study hall for Carol and she wanted to edit the story she had finished that morning, but she couldn't stop thinking about the short conversation that she and David had had after period one. She had turned red in embarrassment. She couldn't help but wonder if he had been serious or merely playing a sick joke to impress his friends. But she hadn't seen anyone around watching. She decided she had to find out and that if she ran into him in the hall, she would ask him.

The bell rang, and she walked out into the hall, where her thought for a second ago came true. She saw David walking down the hall, looking at the floor, thinking. She walked up to him.

"Hello. I am Carol Robinson. We talked earlier this morning and I was wondering if you had been serious about getting together sometime and talking about writing," She said, breathing heavily and shaking.

"Uh, yeah, I was serious. I would love to get together sometime and talk about writing," David said, as nervous as she was.

"Alright," Carol said, taking a breath to relax. "We can talk tomorrow in class and set up a time."

"Yeah, I'll see you then", David said, walking away.

Once at home, Carol went directly to her room. She fell onto her bed and thought about her day. She had went years without talking to one student in that school, and now, on this one particular day, she had made a friend, who just so happened to have the same interests as her.

Carol reached into her backpack, grabbed the story she had finished up that morning, and began editing it. She left her room that night only once, to eat supper. Her mother, Alice, asked her how her first day of high school went, and got a surprising answer.

"It was amazing! I met a guy who also enjoys writing," Carol exclaimed, smiling. "He's really cute."

"Really?" Alice asked, putting down her fork and looking up at her daughter. "That's great! I am so happy for you!"

"Thanks Mom," Carol said, taking her plate over to the sink and going to her bedroom. "See you tomorrow."

"But it's only 7:00. You don't have to be in bed until 9:30," Alice said.

"Yeah but I have a story I am editing and it is going to take me a while." Carol said, turning and facing Alice.

"Alright, I will see you in the morning then. Goodnight," Alice said.

David had put his stuff in his room and gone for a walk as soon as he had gotten home. He needed to think about his story and walking was his best way to do so. He decided to walk to the town park and back to his house.

He thought about his story. He was half done with it now, but the second half was a mystery to him. He thought he might have his main character fall in love with a wealthy woman and move in with her. His other option was to write an interesting conclusion while leaving the poor man still living in the street.

Unfortunately for David, the only thing he could think about was Carol. He couldn't believe that he had made a friend on his first day as a Freshman in high school. He smiled thinking about it, and before he knew it, he had arrived back at home again.

David entered his house and began dinner, because Brenda worked long hours and wouldn't be back until 8:00. He cooked some hot dogs, ate and went to his room to continue working on his story.

David was almost done with his story, when he heard the door open. "David, are you here?" he heard Brenda shout as she closed the door.

"I'm up here!" David yelled, continuing to write. Brenda came up to say hello.

"Hello. I've got to take a shower. I want you in bed no later than ten, alright David?" She asked.

"Okay Brenda," David said. "I'll see you in the morning."

Brenda left the room and David finished his story.

When William returned home, he went directly to his computer and began typing. He rubbed his eyes because he was so tired. He had a deadline to meet, October tenth, and he hadn't even started to make a dent in the story he was writing.

Even with the summer, he had figured it would be fine for him to go out clubbing with friends and picking up chicks, which had seemed like a good idea at the time. Now that the summer was over however, he looked at the computer screen with disbelief.

He couldn't believe that he had only got three pages written. His brain worked furiously to come up with the story. He couldn't believe it. He had been writing his whole life, and he had always been able to come up with stuff on the spot.

But now, he couldn't come up with anything. That night he worked on the story all night, not eating supper and managing to squeeze two paragraphs out, though he wasn't happy with the second one. He yawned, called it a night and went to bed.

CHAPTER 2

William's morning was terrible. He woke up to the phone ringing at 5:30. It was his mother. He told her what time it was to which she responded, "I know, isn't it great William? Ever since I retired, I've been up early enough to enjoy the sunrise. I feel like a new woman."

"That's great mom. I have to get to work, so could we continue this enlightening conversation tonight?" William asked.

Before she answered, he hung up and went to the kitchen. He had no food in the fridge and made a mental note to go to the store after work. He took a shower, almost falling asleep while taking it, got dressed, brushed his teeth and ran out to his car.

He drove down his road quickly to make it to Dunkin Donuts before work. He got a coffee and a few donuts from there and sped off to work. He got half way there before realizing his file for school had been left in his kitchen when he had been looking for breakfast. He did a U Turn and sped back home.

He parked by his driveway, ran back into his house, tripped on a pile of laundry on the floor and hit his head on the wall. He wanted an Asprin, but he didn't have the time. He grabbed his file, ran out to his car and began driving.

He was going ten miles over the limit but he didn't care. He needed to get to work. He looked in his rear view mirror in time to see the cop following him. He sighed and pulled over.

Upon reaching Williams' window, the cop, Officer Ryan Grindle, said "Bill? Why in the name of Sam Hill were you going so fast?"

"Sorry Ryan, I've had a really rough morning," William said.

"You and me both. I had to arrest 3 guys for possession at three this morning", Ryan said. "Not a pretty sight. They didn't just have, they were. And when I say 'were', I mean high as jetliners. I couldn't believe it." Ryan laughed.

"That's fascinating Ryan, but I need to get to the school. Could I please just have my ticket?" William said.

"Oh, right. Here it is. Have a nice day William. I'll see you later, hopefully under better circumstances," Ryan chuckled at his clever remark, got into his car and went on his way.

William drove to the school and went to his classroom. David was waiting for him at the door.

"Oh. Hi, uh, David isn't it? What can I do for you?" William asked, opening his door.

"I don't have anywhere to be, so I was just waiting for you so I could go in and hang out in your room," David said, following William into his room.

"Sure David. Did you finish that assignment?" William asked, making conversation.

"Yeah I did," David said, reaching into his bag. "Here it is." David handed the story to William.

"Cool," William said. "I'll have a look at it right now." William sat down at his desk and took a sip of his coffee than he began reading David's story.

William looked at David and said, "David, this is *very* good. How long have you been writing?"

"Since second grade. I began writing simple things, like about the dreams I had. Then and it led up to original stories, short and then long. It didn't take long for me to realize that I had a true passion for it. I have been writing nonstop ever since," David answered, smiling.

"Well your writing certainly shows your passion. I can tell that you enjoy writing, which is important. I'm a writer. I am currently writing for a magazine," William said.

"So, if you're a writer, why are you a teacher?" David asked, curiously.

"Well, I originally was going to college for an English major, but then I realized that I would probably be writing forever no matter what I did, so I decided to change my major to something that also interested me, which happened to be teaching," William said.

"So are you saying that if I like writing, but I also like something else, I should major in the latter?" David asked.

"Not necessarily. If you like it enough and have enough confidence in your writing that it could actually go somewhere, you should definitely go for an English major," William said. "I admire your curiosity. It's very important to ask questions. Those who don't ask questions, don't get answers, and therefore, don't become smarter."

"Thank you Mr. Morrison. I have always asked lots of questions. I guess I have just always liked to learn," David said.

Then, Carol walked into the room. David smiled.

"Hi," Carol said, walking past William and sitting next to David.

"Hi," David said, smiling.

"Hello Carol," William said, noticing the way that David was looking at Carol. "We were just discussing writing. How long have you been writing?"

"I've been writing for too long to remember. I wrote my first short story in 4th grade. My teacher gave it an instant 'A'. She was speechless," Carol said proudly. "She couldn't believe that a ten year old could write better than she could."

"Very fascinating," Mr. Morrison remarked, looking over at her. "I read your story last night and I was very impressed. I loved the twist ending."

"Thanks, I have always enjoyed movies and books with twist endings and most of my writing has one," Carol said, looking over at David. "What about your writing, do you write twist endings?"

"Most of my stuff is dark and depressing. I'll be the first to admit that I've had a hard life and most of my writing is just me expressing myself, but I have written a few short stories. And when I wrote those stories I found that a happy non twist ending worked for me," David answered, looking at his desk, surprised at what he had just said. He usually didn't tell personal things to people, but he felt comfortable with Carol and William.

"That's cool", Carol said. "I find that a happy ending is much better than some cliffhanger ending. I hate those. Generally, the author keeps you waiting way to long for the next installment, and then it never comes."

William looked over at her. "Funny you should mention cliffhangers, because I am writing a three part mini series for a magazine."

"Really? That's neat. What magazine?" Carol said, smiling.

"Writing Adventures," William said. "I've been writing on and off for them for quite a few years."

"Writing Adventures?" Carol exclaimed. "That's my favorite magazine in the world! When will your first part be published?"

"Hopefully next months issue, but I have to write fast. I still have quite a bit to write for it", William said. "My deadline is next week."

"You can do it!" Carol exclaimed. "I have faith in you."

"Thanks Carol. That's really nice", William said.

David looked up, with a thoughtful look on his face. "So Mr. Morrison, you said you've been writing for a long time. Have you ever considered writing a novel?"

"Actually, I have been writing one on and off for four years. I write some here and there whenever I get the time", William said.

Without notice, the bell rang and the other students began slowly moving into the room. Mr. Morrison looked at the clock. Time had gone very fast. He was surprised. He began going through the file that he had gone back home for and pulled out his syllabus for the day.

When class started, William had the students hand their stories forward, and with the exception with a few students, everyone handed one in. He took them back to his desk and began talking about the assignment.

"Today is, for the most part, going to be a free period. All you need to do is pick a short story to read. Then, you can either start it here, in class or tonight at home. Either way, I expect it to be finished by Wednesday. The short story can be of any genre. There are no limitations. Wednesday, when you all get to school, I will be having you write an essay on why you chose the story, what you thought of the story and such. Now you may find your story and hang out. If you received any homework yesterday that you didn't do, this is a good opportunity to finish it up. If you don't have any homework and you don't want to begin reading in class, you may talk quietly while I grade your stories."

The students all got up and began searching the room's various books for short stories that suited their interests. William noticed that David grabbed an Edgar Allan Poe anthology almost immediately. Carol decided to read O. Henry. She had always been a fan of his and loved how he constructed a story. She decided to read "The Leaf". As soon as she sat back down to her seat, she began reading. David picked out his story, but had no intentions of reading until he got home, for something to do. He picked "The Black Cat" to read.

He had been pondering a story idea through his head all morning and decided to write down some notes for it. The story was about a man whose family had been massacred, so he decided to take action and get revenge on the murderer. He wasn't sure yet how he wanted the murderer to kill the man's family.

Williams' coffee hadn't helped at all. He hadn't started grading the stories, and was sleeping in his chair. Some students had noticed and were throwing things around the room. Then, he awoke suddenly. The students who had been throwing things gasped, but to their surprise, he grabbed a notebook and began writing furiously.

During his quick nap, William had came up with the next scene to part one of the miniseries. All he needed now was the cliffhanger. He wasn't sure where to end the first part, but he needed to make sure that his audience would be waiting for part two.

He wrote as quickly as he could, writing as many notes in as much detail as possible. When he finished, he folded the papers up and put them in his pocket. When he returned home that evening, he would bring the notes out and began writing. He could barely wait. The bell rang, and the students scurried out of the room like lab rats.

William had the next period free and he decided to use the time to go to catch up on sleep.

In the hall, David walked up to Carol and began talking.

"Sorry I didn't talk to you in class", David said. "I'm not great with talking to girls."

"It's alright", Carol said, nervously. "I'm not really great at talking to boys either."

"Hey, if you're not doing anything, I was wondering if you wanted to hang out after school", David said.

"Yeah, sure", Carol said. "I'd like that."

"Okay", David said. "I'll meet you back here after the last period."

"Okay", Carol said, smiling. "Bye."

"Bye", David said, turning to walk to his first class.

When William got home after work, he saw that there was a message on his answering machine and he walked over and pushed the button. The message was from Robert.

"Hey William," Robert's voice said. "I'm having an awesome party tonight at ten o'clock at my place man, you've got to be there. I hope to see you there, I've got to go."

The machine shut off and William thought for a minute. He didn't have anything to correct, and it was Friday night after all. After some careful thinking, he decided to go to the party. He went into his living room and began typing the amazing chapter that he had come up with today.

After his last class ended, David immediately walked to Carol's locker. She was there, waiting for him.

"Hello David", Carol said.

"Hello", David said. "Are you ready?"

"Yes", Carol said. "Where are we going to go?"

"Well, I was thinking we could take a walk", David said. "We could go to the park and swing, if you don't think that's childish."

David felt a bit embarrassed at his idea, but to his surprise, Carol loved it.

"Are you kidding?" Carol said. "I love going to the park."

"Alright", David said, smiling. "Let's go."

They left the school and began walking to the park, which was only a few blocks away.

The town of Bucksport, Maine was very small, but the town's history had helped make it a must see for tourists during the summer time. The population of the townspeople was less than seven thousand, though most of the population was made up of those who had moved there, and not so much those who had grown up there.

The biggest attraction, to those who lived there anyway, was the historic Alamo Theatre. Opened as a place for theatrical performances in the seventeen hundred's, it had now been converted to a movie theater. It was the most popular place to take a first date and, truth be told, the most popular place in town.

The high school was the second most recognized place to the townspeople. It took in students from three surrounding towns, so it had a mixture of people.

The only other popular attraction for the townspeople of Bucksport was a mall, which was actually two towns over. It was the second most popular place for teenagers to go and hang out.

They liked it because, since it was in a different town, it gave them all a sense of freedom being away from their parents.

David and Carol made it to the park and sat down on the swings.

"So, you like writing," David said. "What kind of writing do you like to do?"

"It depends," Carol said. "I like to write romance, but I like a little mystery also."

"That's cool," David said. "I'm more of a horror guy."

"I find that interesting," Carol said.

"In what way?" David asked.

"Horror can be such an expressive genre, from what I've read," Carol said.

"I definitely agree," David said, getting excited. "And apart from all of the monsters and ghosts, horror is in so many ways just a big metaphor for real life and how dark the world really is."

"Oh most definitely," Carol said. "I've always enjoyed reading a horror story from time to time to get my blood pumping,. Sometimes we all just need a good scare from time to time."

"Well maybe sometime you could read one of mine," David said.

"Only if you read one of my romance stories," Carol said.

"It's a deal," David said, extending his hand.

Carol shook his hand back and then they both sat in silence. David sat there, feeling awkward and not knowing what to say.

"So Carol," David said. "I really like you. I…"

Before he could say anymore, Carol was kissing him. He didn't really know what to do, so he embraced her. Honestly, Carol didn't know what she was doing either, but it felt right in the moment. The kiss only lasted five seconds, but it felt like an hour. Being that it was David's first kiss, and Carol's, it felt even more magical than it was.

When it was over, David just sat there, swinging. He was smiling and wondered if Carol was but he was too embarrassed to look.

As Carol sat there, she didn't know why she had kissed David, but she had liked it. Something about David was different than all the other guys she had met. He wasn't popular like all the rest. He was an outcast, just like her.

And they shared the same interests, which was a quality she barely ever found in a male friend. In fact, she hadn't really *had* any male friends. Or female friend, for that matter. After a few minutes, she looked over to David.

"David", Carol said. "I really like you too."

David wasn't really sure what to say. He had never been in this position in his life.

"I'll bet I can swing higher than you," David said, closing his eyes and looking away. He realized how stupid the comment had been, but he couldn't think of anything else to say.

"I'll take that challenge," Carol said, happily erasing the awkward moment.

They swung for another twenty minutes, making small talk. Then they decided that it was time to go home. They began walking away from the park, toward Carol's house.

"Carol," David said. "How would you like to come over to my house tomorrow?"

"Well, it is Saturday," Carol said. "I'll ask my mom. Where do you live?"

"I live on Oak Street," David said. "How about we just meet back at the park and then we can walk to my house."

They got to Carol's house and stopped in front of the driveway. Carol and David turned toward each other.

"Sure," Carol said. She pulled out a pen and paper and wrote something down. "Here's my number. Call me around ten."

"Alright, I will," David said.

"Goodbye David," Carol said, kissing David on the cheek.

"Goodbye Carol," David said, smiling.

William was sitting at his desk, writing vigorously, pushing out paragraph after paragraph, when he looked at his watch. It was 9:30 and he hadn't even began getting ready yet. It was a twenty minute drive to Robert's house and he still needed a quick shower.

He ran into the bathroom and jumped into the shower, barely getting his clothes off and he took an extremely quick shower, for him, which lasted only five minutes. When he got out, he quickly dried off and got dressed again, still slightly wet from the shower. Then he brushed his teeth, grabbed his jacket and ran out the door to his car.

It was now 9:45 and he began driving to Robert's house. He cranked the radio as he drove and made it there in record time.

When William got to Robert's house, he parked his car and walked up to the door. He knocked and after a few seconds, Robert answered.

"Hey man, what's up?" Robert said. "The party's just getting started, I'm glad you could make it."

"Well thanks for inviting me," William said. "I need this party. This miniseries I'm writing is going to kill me."

"Is it going well?" Robert asked.

"Yeah, part one is almost finished, but it's still good to have a break from it," William said.

"I bet", Robert said. "I hardly have any time for writing anymore. I'm always working, which is a real drag."

Robert was a lawyer and hardly ever had time to write, which was what he preferred. He had always figured that if he could get just one book published, he'd be golden, but that hadn't happened yet.

There weren't that many people at the party at first, but William knew that there would be. Robert had always been known for his parties, ever since High School. His parent's were both in business and had to take long trips.

William poured himself a cup of punch, took a sip and began walking around, looking for someone to talk to. After walking around the whole place and finding no one he knew, so he decided to go back and find Robert.

William turned around and ran into a girl who was walking the opposite direction. His punch spilled all over her white dress.

"I am so sorry," William exclaimed. "I'll go get some napkins."

He ran to a near table and grabbed some napkins and ran back to her and began to clean the punch from her dress.

"It's not mine," the girl said.

"What?" William asked, looking at her as he continued to wipe the punch from the dress.

"I borrowed it from a friend," she said. "That way I wouldn't spill anything on mine."

A smile came over her face and she began laughing. William began also, realizing how much of a fuss he had made over spilling the punch.

When they finally stopped laughing, William placed the napkins on a nearby table and looked at the girl. She was gorgeous.

"I'm William Morrison," William said, with a smile, extending his hand.

"I'm Erica Young," She said, shaking his hand.

"Hello Erica," William said. "I don't think I've never seen you at any of Robert's parties before."

"That's because this is my first one," Erica said. "I'm here with my sister."

She pointed across the room.

"Lilly is your sister?" William said. "I didn't know she had one."

"You know Lilly?" Erica asked.

"Yeah," William said. "I went to high school with her."

"I was a year behind her," Erica said.

"Strange," William said. "I don't remember you."

"Well," Erica said. "I spent most of my time in the Library, reading the latest books they got in."

"I see," William said. "I spent most of my time with Robert." He laughed. "I guess not much has changed."

"I guess not," Erica replied. "So what have you been up to since high school?"

"Well, after graduation Robert and I went to college, where we both majored in partying. Of course, they didn't call it that, they called it 'English'. It's a miracle we graduated."

Erica laughed.

"After college I decided to get serious and now I'm an English teacher at Bucksport High School," William said.

"Really?" Erica asked. "I was looking for a job as an English teacher and I was going to apply there."

William smiled, thinking to himself just how good this was to be true. He knew the other teachers but he wasn't what he would call friends with them. Having Erica in the school would be a delight.

"That's an excellent idea", William said. "They have been looking for a new English teacher."

"Have they really?" Erica asked, smiling.

"Yes", William asked. "One of our older English teachers is getting ready to retire and they are looking for a replacement."

"I'll have to stop in Monday morning", Erica said.

"Yes, you should," William said. "Feel free to use me as a reference."

"I'll do that," Erica said, smiling.

"So, what have you been doing since high school," William asked.

"Well, I went to college right after as well," Erica said. "Then I took some time to travel. I went to Colorado for a year and worked at a restaurant. Then I came back home and took a job as an English teacher, but the school that I worked at is doing some serious budget cuts, which is why I am looking for a job now."

"Oh wow," William said. "I've always wanted to travel. Outside a few college road trips, I haven't had a chance to do any traveling."

"That's too bad," Erica said. "Colorado is beautiful if ever get a chance."

She looked at her watch.

"I've got to be going," Erica said.

William looked at his watch as well.

"But it's only nine thirty," William said.

"Yes," Erica said. "But my mother wanted to go shopping tomorrow, and she gets up early, extremely early. She's the kind of person who will show up a half hour earlier than she says and you'd better be ready to go."

"I know the feeling " William said smiling. "My mother calls me every morning, bright and early, whether I'm awake or not."

"Well," Erica said in a sexy voice. "It's been delightful talking to you William. Perhaps I'll get that job so we can see each other more often." She winked at William.

"I hope you do", William said. "That would be great."

Erica said goodbye and turned to walk outside.

William thought for a minute and realized that he didn't want to wait to see if she got the job, he had to see her sooner. As soon as possible. He ran out into the parking lot, hoping to catch her.

When William reached the parking lot, Erica was just getting into her car.

"Erica, wait," William yelled.

Erica stopped her car and rolled down her window as William approached.

"How long are you and your mother going shopping for tomorrow?" William asked, hopeful.

"Well I don't know", Erica said. "We should be back around noon. Why?"

"Well, I was thinking," William said. "Would you like to go out to dinner with me tomorrow night?"

"I would love to", Erica said, smiling. "I'll give you my number."

She wrote down her number and handed it to William.

"Well alright," William said. "I'll give you a call around noon."

"Alright William", Erica said. "Goodnight."

"Goodnight Erica", William said as she drove away.

William folded up Erica's number and put it into his pocket. Then he walked to his car, deciding to go home before the party got really wild. It always seemed like everything was alright until about eleven o'clock and then, no matter what, Robert's parties always seemed to go a bit hay-wire.

William drove home, not believing that he had met a beautiful woman. Usually the girls he ended up, especially the ones he met at Robert's parties, with weren't exactly what one would call beautiful. They seemed to have a wild look to them and they were more up Robert's alley than William's.

William decided to go home and watch a bit of TV and relax, since he didn't have to worry about writing for a while.

Erica pulled into her driveway and walked inside, grinning ear to ear the whole time.

He's amazing, Erica thought as she poured herself a small glass of wine. She sat down in her living room chair. She sipped her wine as she looked outside, watching the cars go by.

She recalled her exes, and how two of them had just been blind dates set up by Lilly that she only stayed with because she was afraid of being alone.

William was definitely different from all of her past boyfriends. For one, and the one that made her chuckle out loud at the realization, he was the only one with a clear career path. And for another, he was actually nice. She could tell that it wasn't just an act.

And the fact that he was friends with Robert said something to her too. It was true that Robert was a notorious party animal, but at the core, he was also one of the nicest people on the planet.

She took a final sip of wine and she stood up. She put the glass in the sink and walked into her bedroom. She put on some soothing piano music, took off her clothes and got into bed. She fell asleep to have soothing dreams about William and her first date, which she was sure would be a wonderful occasion.

CHAPTER 3

When David woke up, he rubbed his eyes and looked at his clock and saw that it was already nine thirty. He jumped out of and pulled his clothes on. He ran into the bathroom and brushed his hair and teeth. He wanted to look his best for Carol. He had already asked Brenda if Carol could come over and she had said yes.

He looked in the mirror and began laughing out loud.

"I think you went a bit overboard with the whole 'looking good for Carol' thing," He said to himself.

He was staring at his reflection, which featured him in a full tuxedo that he hadn't worn for months. He finished up in the bathroom and walked back to his room to change into something a little more casual.

Carol had said to call her around ten, and it was nine forty-five. David decided that it was close enough. After he finished changing, he practically ran to the living room and grabbed the phone, Carol's number in hand and dialed her number. He prayed that she would answer.

Carol answered the phone with an enthusiastic "Hi".

"Hi Carol", David said shakily. "Did your mom say you could come over?"

"Yeah, she actually said she can give me a ride over in twenty minutes, if that's alright," Carol said.

"Great," David practically yelled. "I'll meet you outside."

"Okay, where do you live?" Carol asked.

"I live at 14 Maple Road," David said.

"Alright, I'll see you soon," Carol said, in an excited voice. "Goodbye."

"Goodbye Carol," David said, smiling from ear to ear.

David went into the kitchen where Brenda was eating some eggs and drinking coffee.

"Good morning David", Brenda said. "I made an egg for you. It should still be warm."

"Alright Brenda, thank you," David said. "Carol will be here in about twenty minutes."

"Okay," Brenda said, smiling. "I'm so happy that you've made a friend, David."

"Thank you", David said, walking over to the frying pan and putting the egg on a plate. He grabbed a fork and walked over to the table.

He ate the egg and then looked at the clock. Carol would be arriving soon. He decided to walk out and wait for her on the porch.

Carol was extremely nervous, but she was just as excited. She had never gone to a boy's house before, and the fact that she liked David, maybe enough to date him, made it that much more exciting.

A car pulled into David's driveway. David looked up from staring at the ground to see who it was. He saw Carol smiling at him from the driver's seat.

Carol opened the door and hopped out.

"I'll pick you up at five," Alice said as Carol got out.

"Alright," Carol said. "I love you Mom."

"I love you too Carol," Alice said, smiling at her daughter and then at David.

David walked over to meet her.

"David, this is my mom, Alice," Carol said. "Mom, this is David."

"Hi," David said. "How do you do?"

"I do very well," Alice said, smiling. "You two have a nice day."

"Thank you," David said.

Alice pulled out of the driveway and David turned to Carol.

"Hello," David said, hugging Carol.

"Hello," Carol said, hugging him back.

Hugging David brought a smile to Carol's face, and made her blush a little. David turned around and took her hand. He led her into his house, where Brenda was still at the table. David led Carol over to her.

"Brenda, this is Carol. Carol, this is my foster mother Brenda," David said proudly.

"It's nice to meet you Carol," Brenda said.

"It's nice to meet you too," Carol said, smiling.

"Well," David said. "What would you like to do?"

"Actually, I printed off one of my stories this morning," Carol said. "And I was thinking that you could read one of mine and I could read one of yours."

"That's a great idea," David said. "I'll print one off for you now. My room's this way."

David took her hand again and led her into his room.

"Sorry it's so messy," David said.

"It's alright," Carol said. "Believe it or not, mines worse."

They shared a short laugh.

"It must just be a teenager thing," David said, laughing. "Make yourself comfortable. I'll go through my documents and find a good story to print off.

David found one and printed it off. He picked it up from his printer and walked over to Carol.

"Here it is," David said.

"I can't wait to read it," Carol said, excited. "Here's the one I picked for you."

They traded and David laid down next to Carol on his bed. They got close and they began reading.

Carol's story was called "Some Kind of Love" and was about a divorced woman who finds love after five years of searching for someone new. David's story was called "The Game of Death" and was about a serial killer who had set up his killings so that they were all connected to a man who would be his final victim.

The stories were quite different, but David and Carol were both too excited to read to even notice.

David finished Carol's story first and he set it down.

"That was amazing," David said, looking at Carol and smiling. "I never knew that romance could be so beautiful, though I suppose that's the point."

Carol looked up, also smiling. She didn't know why but she had a feeling inside her. She couldn't explain it, but it was the most awesome feeling she had ever felt. Whenever she looked at David, she felt it and suddenly she wanted to embrace him.

Carol quickly finished David's story and put it down. She hugged him.

"David, I've never been a fan of horror, but you write it so beautifully, if that's possible," Carol said. "I want to see more of you, I mean more of your writing." Carol blushed.

"I want to read more of your writing also," David said, a small smile coming across his face.

Before he even thought about it, David's mouth was connected to Carol's. An autumn breeze flowed through the window, which made them pull closer together for warmth. Within what seemed like seconds, their clothes were off and David was on top of Carol.

Ten minutes later, Carol stood up. She pulled on her shirt, and just stood there, staring at David. She was happy, but she didn't know how to express it. The whole situation brought her back to the nervous yet excited feeling that she had felt before she got here.

David stood up and kissed her neck.

"Do you want some lunch?" David asked.

He closed his eyes hard, nervous that Carol would want to go home.

"I'd love some", Carol said, smiling slyly at David.

David was surprised, but he took her hand and led her out to the kitchen. Brenda had gone to work and the kitchen and living room were both silent.

David got some bread and pulled out some ham and mayo from the refrigerator.

"Is a ham sandwich alright?" David asked.

"Yes," Carol said quietly. "It's my favorite."

Carol was still in a bit of a daze, trying to figure out if she was dreaming. All that she knew for sure was that if this was a dream, it was the greatest dream she had ever had. An overwhelming feeling had come over her and for a couple of seconds, she had trouble breathing. She realized what she had just done with David, and accepted it. The daze went away and she looked up at David, who was still making their sandwiches.

David made them each a sandwich and put them on plates. Then he put one in front of Carol and sat down next to her.

They ate in silence for the most part. David opened his mouth a few times to say something, but he closed it each time. He couldn't find the right words.

Like Carol, he didn't really know how to handle the situation. The only time he had ever been in a similar situation was when he was younger and had made out with his foster sister. It hadn't amounted to anything and they had both felt awkward afterward. But he had never done anything like this before.   David was struggling to find the words to say, and wondered if he should say anything. Finally, Carol put down her sandwich, swallowed hard and looked at David.

"I love you, David", Carol said in one breath. "And not just because of what happened, you're the nicest person I know and one of the only friends I've ever had."

"I love you too Carol," David said without thought. "I just don't want that to change anything."

"Me neither," Carol said. "I just want to be with you."

"Good," David said. "Then we can just pretend it didn't happen."

David got a thoughtful look on his face. "Was I good?"

He smiled and they both began laughing out loud.

Carol didn't say anything, but he could tell by the look in her eyes that the answer was 'yes'.

After lunch, David and Carol went back into David's room and laid back down on his bed. They embraced one another and went to sleep.

They woke up at four thirty and they got out of bed. David looked at his clock and realized that they had half an hour before Alice would be there to pick up Carol. He suddenly felt sad that she had to leave, but the fact that he would see her again soon made it better.

David led Carol out onto the porch and sat down on the steps. They made small talk until Alice pulled into the driveway.

David and Carol stood up and walked over to the car. Carol hugged David and he hugged her back.

"I love you," David whispered into Carol's ear as he let her go.

"I love you too David," Carol whispered back, smiling.

William had called Erica at noon and he had got her address. He had let her pick the restaurant, after a lengthy dispute about prices. He had told her that he didn't care about prices, but she had been hesitant for a while.

Finally, she picked Eastman's, a family owned place on Main Street. William had said alright, and told her that he would pick her up around six o'clock. Now it was five thirty and he was just headed out to his car, Erica's address in hand.

He knew where the road was, but he wasn't sure of the house. He found the house in only a few minutes, which made him feel silly because he had left the house half an hour early.

William got out of his car and walked up to the door and knocked.

Erica came to the door, wearing a beautiful blue dress. She had hoped that William would be dressed up, which he was, because she would have felt silly if he wasn't.

"Hello Erica, you look beautiful", William said. "Are you ready?"

"Yes I am", Erica said, "Just let me get my purse."

"Alright", William said. He waited in the doorway until she returned. She then stepped out and closed the door.

William led her around to the passenger side and opened the door for her. She got in and he closed the door. Then he walked around and got in the drivers side.

Eastman's was a busy place, especially on the weekend, but William didn't care because all he cared about was making Erica happy. He had just met her, but he didn't care. He had felt an immediate connection as soon as they had began talking.

When they got to Eastman's, William opened Erica's door for her and took her arm. He led her up the stairs and opened the door. Then, they walked over to the front desk.

"Two?" The woman at the desk asked.

"Yes," William said, holding back a smart ass remark.

"This way please," the woman said, picking up two menus and walking towards a table.

The woman stopped at a table and William and Erica sat down.

"A waitress will be with you shortly," she said.

"Thank you," William said.

"I'm so excited," Erica said, when the woman had walked away.

"Why?" William asked curiously.

"Well, to be honest," Erica said. "I haven't been on a date for quite some time."

"I haven't either," William said, figuring that one night stands wouldn't count. "But not for the lack of trying."

"Well I'm glad that I'm here with you," Erica said. "You seem so sweet."

"Oh, I *seem* sweet," William said, smiled. "I'm not sweet?"

"Well I don't know you that well," Erica said, laughing.

"Well, I like to think that I'm pretty sweet," William said.

Then, a waitress walked over to the table.

"Hello, my name is Kayla, I'll be your waitress tonight," She said. "May I start you off with some beverages?"

"I'll have water," William said.

"I'll have the same," Erica said, smiling.

"Alright," Kayla said. "I'll be back to take your order."

"I haven't even looked at this menu yet," William said as Kayla walked away.

"Me neither," Erica said, picking up her menu. "But it all looks so good."

"Yeah it does," William said. "I think I'll have steak and potatoes."

"That sounds good," Erica said. "I'll have that too."

William smiled at Erica.

"You're beautiful," William said, blushing once he realized that he had said it out loud.

"Thank you," Erica said. "You're pretty cute yourself."

Kayla came back with their water and took their order and then in only a short time, she brought their meals.

"Wow," William said. "The service here is amazing."

"Yeah," Erica said. "The best I've ever seen at a restaurant."

William began laughing hysterically.

"What?" Erica asked.

"Nothing," William said. "It's just that we sound like we're reading the script to a bad movie."

Erica nodded and began laughing as well.

"This steak tastes *really* great," Erica said, in an exaggerated tone.

"I know," William said, also in an exaggerated tone. "It's *so* juicy."

They both burst into laughter again.

"I'm having a really good time," Erica said.

"I'm glad," William said. "I'm having a really good time too. Do you think we can do this again sometime soon?"

"I think that could be arranged," Erica said. "The sooner the better."

They smiled at each other.

"I agree," William said.

They both finished their food, making small talk and laughing while they ate. After paying, they left the restaurant and got into William's car.

William drove Erica home and parked in her driveway.

"Erica," William said. "You are the most gorgeous woman I have ever seen."

"That's the nicest thing anyone has ever said to me," Erica said.

"Well it's true," William said, almost in a whisper.

William leaned in and so did Erica. Their lips connected and suddenly nothing mattered. In the brief time that they were kissing, time seemed to stop.

When it was over, they were both stunned and breathing heavily.

"Goodnight," Erica said. "Call me soon." She winked as she opened the door.

"Goodnight Erica," William said.

Smiling, Erica walked toward her house, shaking from the happiness.

William went through his CD case and put John Mellencamp into his CD player because he felt as though he was back in high school.

CHAPTER 4

In October, William and Erica became extremely close. Erica had applied and got the job at Bucksport High School. Her room was across the hall from William's, so they got to see each other as often as they wanted.

Carol and David started talking all the time and spent as much time together as possible. Every day, when it was possible, they hung out after school.

David had promised Carol a date, but he hadn't figured out when. Since he had never had a girlfriend, he had no dating experience whatsoever and he didn't know when or where to take her.

From what he had seen in romantic made-for-TV movies, he assumed that taking her to the local movie theater would be a good start. The problem was that there hadn't been a good 'date worthy' movie playing there since David and Carol had started hanging out.

On the third weekend of October however, the theater was showing the perfect movie, a romance.

It was Friday, and the bell had just rang. David ran to Carol's locker to tell her the good news. He was so excited that he almost tripped.

David got to Carol's locker as she was putting her homework in her backpack.

"Carol," David said, as he approached her. "How would you like to go to the movies with me tonight?"

"I would love to," Carol said, smiling. "What time is it?"

"It's at six thirty," David said.

"Alright," Carol said. "I'm going to go home and get ready. I'll see if mom can drive us there."

"Sounds good," David said. "I'll walk you out."

David walked Carol outside and to the end of the school's driveway. Carol's house was to the left and David's was to the right, so they walked to the end together and on days when they didn't hang out, they went their separate ways.

"I'll see you tonight," David said, leaning in to kiss Carol.

Carol kissed him back.

"See you tonight. I love you," Carol said.

"I love you too," David said, turning and walking away.

Carol thought about what she would wear the entire walk home. She hadn't ever been on a date before and she didn't know what she should wear. She decided that she would ask Alice when she got home.

When Carol walked through the door, Alice was watching TV drinking ice tea.

"Mom," Carol said with a deep breath. "I have a date tonight."

Alice looked up and smiled.

"That's great," Alice exclaimed.

"Thanks," Carol said. "David is taking me to the movies. I was wondering if you could help me figure out what to wear?"

"Definitely," Alice said, standing up. "This is a special occasion. You need to wear a dress."

"A dress?" Carol asked. "Are you serious?"

"Hon, it's your first date, you want to look nice," Alice said.

"Yeah, I want to look nice," Carol said. "Not old."

"You won't look 'old' in a dress. Wearing dresses didn't go out when I was in high school," Alice said. "But if you don't want to wear one, I'll let you borrow a nice shirt?"

"That sounds better," Carol said.

"Alright," Alice said. "I'll go get it."

Alice went into her room and came back out holding a blue shirt that had some ruffles.

"I know it looks fancy, but it's all I've got," Alice said. "I wore this to your Aunt Jane's wedding."

"Its fine," Carol said, taking the shirt. "I'm sure he'll love it."

When he got home, David told Brenda about his date, and she congratulated him and told him about the first date she had ever gone on, when she was a sophomore in high school.

"It was magical," Brenda told him. "He took me to a small, family owned diner. It was the cheapest place in town, but it's all he could afford. I remember that we both got tuna fish sandwiches and soda's. We didn't talk very much the whole time, but it was one of the magical nights of my life. It was also the night I got my first kiss. I think that the most magical part about any first date is the first kiss that you share with someone."

"Yeah, I bet," David said, thinking of how he and Carol would not be able to have that memory of their first date.

"We dated for the rest of high school," Brenda said. "But after that, we went to separate colleges and didn't get to see much of each other. Rumor even had it that he had cheated on me, but who knows? The fact was that we weren't meant to be."

Brenda took in a deep, thoughtful breath, thinking of her first relationship. Her thoughts were broken as David chimed in.

"I forgot, Brenda, I'm going to need some money, if that's alright," David said hopefully.

"Yes, you can have some money for your first date," Brenda said, still smiling. "Treat her right, and above all, have a good time!"

Brenda had given him enough to get tickets and some popcorn.

David didn't know whether or not to go casual or if he should dress up. He decided that perhaps it would be better to change his clothes, but still go casual. He didn't want Carol to think he was weird. He picked out some clothes that were slightly fancy, but not so much that they could not be considered casual.

David went into the bathroom and took a shower, so he would be clean for a night which he was sure he would remember for his entire life.

The phone rang at five forty-thirty and David heard Brenda pick it up.

"David, it's Carol," Brenda called.

David sprinted out into the kitchen and took the phone.

"Hello," David said, catching his breath.

"Hello David," Carol said. "We're on our way."

"Alright," David said. "I'll see you in a few minutes."

David said goodbye to Brenda and walked out onto the porch to wait for Carol and Alice.

Alice's car pulled into the driveway and she parked. Carol got out of the car and David almost choked when he saw her. He walked over to her in awe.

"You look beautiful," David said to Carol.

"Thank you David," Carol said. "You look nice too."

"Sorry," David said. "I wasn't sure what to wear."

"Its fine," Carol said. "I wasn't sure either."

Carol opened up the door and they both got in. They buckled their seat belts and Alice backed out of the driveway and headed to the movie theater.

The movie theater was only a few minutes away. Alice dropped them off in the front and said that she would be back around eight. They said goodbye to her and went inside.

"This is going to be fun," David said, while they were in line.

"Yeah I know," Carol said. "I'm so happy you asked me."

"Well why wouldn't I?" David asked. "You're the most beautiful girl in the world."

"Thank you so much," Carol said, practically crying with joy.

"My pleasure," David said.

They had made their way to the front of the line and David paid for their tickets and got a large popcorn. Then they walked into the theater.

"Where do you want to sit?" David asked.

"In the front row," Carol said, leading the way.

"Cool," David said. "I've never sat in the front before."

They sat down and began talking.

"Why not," Carol asked.

"I don't really know," David said. "I just usually sit in the back."

"Do you come here often?" Carol asked.

"Yeah," David said. "It's my home away from home. And I usually sit in the back where I'm away from most everyone else."

"Oh," Carol said. "I like being up front. It makes you feel like you're part of the movie."

The movie started and they both looked up at the screen. David moved his hand over and found Carol's. They both looked at each other and smiled. David leaned in and they had the most passionate kiss of either of their lives so far.

It lasted five minutes, longer than any of theirs had. When it was over, David pulled Carol close to him and they watched the rest of the movie.

When the movie was over, David and Carol walked outside. It was raining hard, and Alice wasn't there yet.

"Carol," David said. "I really love you. I have never felt this way about anyone before in my life."

"I've never felt this way about anyone either," Carol said.

They hugged, getting soaked in the pouring rain. They held each other close, breathing slowly until Alice got there.

When Alice pulled up, they got into her car and she took David home. Alice got out and gave David a hug and a kiss.

"Bye David," Carol said. "I love you."

"I love you too, Carol," David said. "I'll call you tomorrow."

"Okay," Carol said, getting into the car.

"So," Alice said, when Carol closed the door. "How was the date?"

"It was amazing," Carol said.

"I'm glad you had a good time," Alice said, smiling. "I know you already watched a movie tonight, but I rented one for us to watch tonight in celebration of your first date."

"What movie?" Carol asked.

"Grease," Alice said. "Our favorite."

"You're the best," Carol yelled.

"I try my best," Alice said, laughing.

When they got home, Carol and Alice went inside and made some popcorn. Then they sat down in the living room and watched *Grease*.

CHAPTER 5

William sat at his desk and stared at his picture of Erica. In his hand, he held two keys, both to his front door. He knew that they had only been dating for a little while, but he knew that he would never find anyone else like her.

He had always hated the cliché, but he didn't care. He knew that she was 'the one'. He could feel it. He loved her with such a passion that it made him hot just to think about her. Finally, he stood up. He took a deep breath and walked over to his phone. He picked it up and dialed Erica's number.

"Hello," Erica answered.

"Hello, Erica," William said. "How are you doing?"

"I'm doing good," Erica said. "What's up?"

"I was wondering if you wanted to go out tonight," William said.

"I'd love to," Erica said. "Where were you thinking of going?"

"I was thinking dinner and a movie," William said, hitting his head against a wall at how generic that was. He had taken her to out to dinner and then to a movie every time they had gone out. He feared that if he didn't find somewhere else soon that she would leave him, but there wasn't anything else to do in such a small town. Suddenly, he remembered that it was Friday and that there was a football game that night. His eyes bolted open and he smiled wide.

"Actually," William said. "Let's go to the football game."

"Oh, I would love to," Erica said. "I love football."

"Really," William asked. "Great, I'll pick you up at seven thirty. The game's at eight."

"Okay," Erica said. "I love you."

"I love you too, Erica," William said. He hung up the phone and let out a sigh of relief.

"Nice save, Morrison," He said as he walked back over to his desk and started typing.

David and Carol had also made plans to go to the football game. David had asked Brenda if she would take them and she said yes. David and Brenda were going to pick Carol up at seven forty five and they were going to go straight to the game.

David picked out a plain white t shirt so that he would look nice for the date. He went out into the kitchen and sat down at the table. Brenda handed him his plate and he began to eat the spaghetti she had made. He ate so quickly that he didn't even think about the delicious food he was putting into his mouth. This was the first time that he had taken Carol out anywhere but a restaurant and the movies.

After he finished eating, he called Carol and told her that they were on their way. Brenda and David walked outside and got in the car. They pulled out of the driveway and started to drive to Carol's house.

It was a beautiful October night. There was a lovely autumn smell in the air. The sky was a dark blue with sparkling stars scattered all over. The trees swayed as they drove past them.

They pulled into Carol's driveway and David jumped out and ran to the door. He knocked and Carol opened the door.

"Hey," Carol said.

"Hi," David said. He kissed her and she looked back inside.

"Bye mom," Carol said.

"Bye Carol, goodbye David," Alice yelled.

"Goodbye," David yelled back. They walked to the car and David opened up the back seat door for Carol. Once she was in, he ran to the other side of the car and got in.

While they rode to the football game, David held Carol's hand tight in his. They smiled at each other and Carol opened her mouth to say something, but she didn't. Something in her throat stopped her. It was so silly, childish even.

"What is it?" David asked.

"I just wanted to say thank you," Carol said. "For taking me to the game tonight, I mean."

"It's my pleasure," David said.

"I know," Carol said. "I've just never been to a football game here because I never had anyone to go with."

"Well now you do," David said.

Carol smiled and leaned over and put her head on David's shoulder for the rest of the ride.

It was seven o'clock and William grabbed his coat and walked outside and got into his car. He had just finished the story he had been writing and submitted it.

He had edited it three times personally and he had even had his good friend and high school English teacher edit it. The best part was that it was done five days early.

He hummed along with the radio as he drove to Erica's house. He was so proud of his story. Now he could finally get back to his novel that he had been writing when he got the job to write the story.

He pulled into Erica's driveway and shut off his car. He got out, walked up to the front door and knocked.

Erica opened up her door and smiled.

"Hi," Erica said. "I'm almost ready I just have to finish drying my hair. Have a seat in the living room."

"Okay," William said.

William walked into her living room. He sat down in her recliner and looked around. It was a nice place, but he still hoped that she would accept his offer tonight and come live with him.

The thought made him smile to himself and even chuckle out loud. It seemed so ridiculous, even to him. He really wanted her to accept, but he couldn't help but feel nervous. He had already prepared himself for rejection, and hoped that if she did say no, it would not result in the end of their relationship.

Thinking about living with Erica made William's heart feel warm and he breathed in and out and smiled. He got so caught up in thinking, that he didn't even see Erica come into the living room.

"Okay," Erica said. "I'm ready."

"Huh," William said, coming back to reality. "Oh, alright let's go."

They walked outside and got into his car.

Brenda dropped David and Carol off at the game and went back home. They walked to the ticket booth. David paid the eight dollars and they went to find a seat. Tonight, the home team the Bucksport Golden Bucks, were playing against their rivals, the Vikings.

"I love football," Carol said, excitement in her eyes.

"I prefer basketball," David said. "But anything you like, I like."

Carol smiled and leaned in for a kiss. The kiss lasted until the game started.

The stands from both sides erupted with yelling and hollering. "Let's go, Bucks!" and "Let's do it!" were among the many yells and chants being yelled.

The yelling was endless throughout the entire game.

"David," Carol yelled over the roar of the crowd. "Would you like to go walk around the track?"

"Yes," David replied, smiling.

They got up and walked down the stairs, passing William and Erica. The four of them exchanged 'hello's' and David and Carol continued walking.

"Erica, I have something to ask you," William said, so quietly that Erica could barely hear him at first.

She leaned in closer and said, "What is it?"

"Just so you know, if you say no I'll understand. I mean, it is kind of sudden," William stammered. He kept speaking, but he couldn't seem to get the right words out.

"William, you seem so nervous," Erica said. "What is it?"

William quickly reached into his pocket and pulled out the key.

"Erica," William said, a terrified look on his face. "Would you like to move in with me?"

At first, Erica was speechless. She had expected a piece of jewelry, but nothing like this. Finally, she smiled, her eyes tearing up, and she spoke.

"Yes," Erica said, taking the key. "I would love that!"

She embraced William and kissed him more passionately than she ever had.

"I'm so happy," William said, after the kiss. "I was so scared that you would say no."

"It was kind of obvious," Erica said, smiling.

"Really," William said, also smiling.

"Just a bit," Erica said. Then they both laughed. William put his arm around Erica and pulled her close to him.

The track went around the whole football field. David and Carol stood in the middle of each of the stands, giving them a great view of the game. They were cuddled up, leaning against the fence.

"So I was talking to my mom earlier," Carol said. "And I asked her if you could stay the night."

"What did she say?" David said, eagerly.

"She said yes," Carol said, smiling.

"That's awesome," David said, in shock. "I'll ask Brenda when she comes to pick us up."

The game ended with a Black Bear victory, 65-45. David and Carol walked to the parking lot, where Brenda was waiting for them.

They walked over and got into the car.

"Brenda, can I stay over at Carol's house tonight?" David asked.

"If it's alright with Carol's mom, it's alright with me," Brenda said.

"It is," Carol said. "I asked her today."

"Okay then," Brenda said. "We'll stop by the house so you can get a change of clothes, okay David?"

"Alright," David said, smiling at Carol.

Soon, they pulled into David's driveway and David ran inside and grabbed some clothes and his toothbrush.

When they got to Carol's house, David said, 'bye' to Brenda and Carol and him walked inside.

Alice greeted them when they got inside and asked them about the football game. They told her about the victory and went into Carol's room.

"You can put your things over there," Carol said, pointing to a chair in the corner.

David walked over to the chair and set his things down.

Then he walked over and sat on Carol's bed, where she was holding a few movies.

"Which one should we watch?" Carol said.

"We're going to watch a movie?" David asked, smiling slyly.

"For a minute, at least," Carol said, giggling.

David chose one called, *Baby Love* and Carol put it in. They watched for a few minutes and David gently touched Carol's cheek and moved her face toward his. A cold chill went up David's back as they slowly laid down on her bed.

"Can we close the window," Erica said. "It's cold in here."

"Sure, babe," William said.

He got up from the bed and walked over to the window. He closed it and walked back over.

"You're the best," He said to Erica, kissing her. "Do you want another glass of champagne before we go to sleep?"

"Sure," Erica said, lifting her glass. He filled her glass and then his. He lifted his glass in a toast.

"To us," William said. "And to all the good things to come."

"To us," Erica said, raising her glass to his.

CHAPTER 6

Carol and David woke up around eleven o'clock and went into the kitchen. Carol made them each a sandwich and they ate lunch.

"Last night was amazing," Carol said, after realizing that Alice had already gone to work.

"I know," David said. "I have to say something though."

"What?" Carol asked.

"I love you, Carol," David said. "And I don't want our relationship to become purely about sex."

"I totally agree," Carol said. She leaned over and hugged David. "So what do you want to do today?"

"I don't know," David said. "We should do something though."

"I agree," Carol said, smiling. "But what?"

"Well, my dear," David said, smiling back. "I'm not sure. We could watch TV and go to dinner and a movie tonight."

"I hate small towns," Carol said, laughing. "But unfortunately, that's all we have to do. It sounds like fun."

"Okay," David said, laughing.

They finished their lunch and walked into the living room. Carol grabbed the remote and they cuddled up on the couch and began watching television.

They had been watching for about a half hour, when Carol jumped up and ran for the bathroom. She began to vomit when she got in there.

William was at Erica's house helping her pack her things into boxes. He was still in a daze, not believing that she had actually said that she would move in with him. He loved her so much. He had never loved anyone as much as he loved Erica. He smiled as he lifted a box full of her clothes and carried it out to his car.

"I invited our parents to have supper tonight," Erica said. "Is that alright?"

"Yeah," William said. "That's a great idea." He wrapped his arms around her and kissed her.

"That's a load," William said. "Let's head to the house and unload it."

They got into the car and started heading for William's house.

"I hate moving," Erica said, once they were on the road. "No offense, I've always hated moving."

"I understand," William said. "It's such a hassle. But this time it's worth it."

"Yes it will," Erica said, smiling. "But luckily this is the last place I plan on moving." She reached over and held William's hand. He pulled her hand up and kissed it. They were both so happy, and they continued holding hands for the remainder of the ride.

"Carol," David said, standing outside the bathroom door. "Is everything alright?"

There was silence for a minute, then David heard the toilet flush and the door opened.

"Yeah," Carol said, stepping out. "I'm fine I must have a stomach virus or something." She forced a smile.

"Are you sure?" David asked.

"I don't know," Carol said. She then added, very quickly, "David, I love you."

"I love you too," David said. David wasn't sure how he felt about this situation. Carol was acting a bit odd. But he forced a smile anyway.

Carol looked up. "Would you mind leaving?" Carol asked.

"If you want," David said, his smile fading. "Did I do something?"

"No," Carol said. "I just want to be alone. I'll call you later, okay?"

"Okay," David responded.

David silently got his things and put on his shoes. He didn't mind walking home, what bothered him was how Carol was acting. Why would she suddenly want him to leave? She had said that she might have a stomach virus, but that was no reason for David to leave. She said that she just wanted him to leave. He pondered all of these thoughts as he walked home.

He began getting paranoid about what this all meant. He was jogging his memory as well as he possibly could, trying to think of *anything* he had said that may have upset her.

The only thing we've talked about lately was about how we didn't want our relationship to be entirely about sex, David thought. *It's impossible that the idea made her mad, isn't it? Is it possible that she just wants sex? That's stupid, that can't be it.*

David walked inside and walked up to his room, these thoughts still in his mind and some still developing. He didn't know why women did the things they did, or why they said the things that they did.

If this had been a movie, David would suspect that he had done nothing wrong, that nothing was really wrong, and that this was just the way that women acted. But this was no movie, and David was smarter than that.

He decided that the best thing to do was to just take his mind off of things altogether. He had been thinking about writing a new story, and he decided that since it was Sunday, he would to start it. He got a notebook and a pencil and began to write, leaving the real problems in the real world and beginning some new ones in the fictional world.

After they had moved about half of Erica's things, William and Erica decided to take the rest of the day off. They would get the rest of it throughout the week after work.

Their parents got to the house around seven o'clock. William had cooked a ham and potatoes for supper and an apple pie for desert.

Erica showed her and William's parents to the table as William got the ham out of the oven. He brought it to the table and set it down.

"I'm just going to get the potatoes, I'll be right back," William said. He wouldn't admit it, but he was very nervous. This was his first time meeting Erica's parents and also the first time that his parents were going to meet Erica.

William got the potatoes and had Erica bring in a bottle of wine.

"What's this?" Kathleen, William's mother said.

"It's wine, mom," William said.

"Didn't I teach you anything?" Kathleen said. "It's brandy or nothing." She laughed.

"Well," William said, turning red. "I thought it would be nice for dinner."

William finished pouring the wine and sat down.

"Well," William said. "Has everyone gotten a chance to meet?"

When nobody moved a muscle, William decided to introduce everyone.

"Mom, Dad, this is Erica," William said.

"Hello," Erica said, shaking their hands. "This is Carl and Mona, my parents."

All four parents took their turns shaking hands.

"My name is Stephen and this is my wife Kathleen," Stephen, William's father said, chuckling. "And this is my son, William."

William's face turned red again, realizing that he hadn't introduced himself, nonetheless his own parents by name.

Carl and Mona chuckled.

"No need to get embarrassed, William," Carl said. "It's quite alright. So, you're the man who has made my daughter so happy."

"I suppose I am," William said.

"Well," Mona said happily. "It's nice to finally meet you."

"It's nice to finally meet you too," William said.

Erica and William's parents made the same exchange and they finally began eating.

"This is great ham," Carl said.

"Thank you," William said. "There's an apple pie for desert."

"You cooked this?" Mona asked.

William shook his head and Kathleen chimed in.

"Oh yes," Kathleen said. "William has always enjoyed cooking. He used to always help out in the kitchen."

"Mom, please," William said, and then Stephen chimed in.

"Can't you leave him alone for one second," Stephen said. "Can't you see he's embarrassed enough as it is?"

"There's nothing to be embarrassed about, William," Carl said. "Some of the best cooks are men. Why didn't you go into culinary school?"

"I was going to," William said, ignoring his father. "But I wanted something a little more close to home."

"That's very nice," Mona said.

"Yes," Kathleen said. "He's always been a nice boy."

"Leave him the hell alone," Stephen yelled.

"Dad, have you been drinking today?" William asked.

"No, I haven't. Why do you ask?" Stephen said.

"Never mind," William said. "I was just wondering."

"So," Mona said. "Do you plan on having children?"

"*MOM!*" Erica yelled.

"I just want to know," Mona said.

"Who wants pie?" William said, standing up.

"We haven't finished our meal yet," Stephen said.

"Take it with you, Dad," William said.

William quickly served the pie and ended the night as quickly as possible.

"Well," Erica said when everyone had left. "It wasn't a *complete* disaster."

William looked at her and they started laughing, uncontrollably. They walked into William's room and went to bed.

David didn't see or hear anything from Carol until he got to Mr. Morrison's room the next morning. He got out of his seat and walked over to her.

"Hey, Carol," David said cheerfully.

Carol didn't say a word. Instead she reached into her backpack and pulled out a piece of paper. She handed the paper to David and looked down. David walked slowly back to his seat, confused. He opened the paper and began reading.

"David," the note read. *"I'm sorry I haven't called you since yesterday. I don't know how to say this, which is why I'm writing it. I think I'm pregnant, David. My mom's buying me a pregnancy test today and I'll do it after school. I just want to be alone today."*

David sat at his desk, his jaw dropped. He looked over towards Carol, who was silently staring at the floor.

"Carol," William said, walking over to her. "Are you alright?"

"I'll be alright, Mr. Morrison," Carol said. "Thank you for your concern."

"Alright," William said, unconvinced. He walked slowly back to his desk and sat down.

The bell rang, and despite the fact that his first class was with William, David stood up and stormed out of the room. He ran into an older student, Alan.

"Watch where you're going, asshole," yelled Alan.

David turned around, fist balled up, and punched Alan in the face. Alan fell hard, but got up quickly and grabbed David by the neck and slammed him into a locker. David kicked hard, but it didn't faze Alan at all.

William walked out of his classroom to see what was going on.

"Hey," William yelled. "What's going on?"

William walked over and pulled Alan away from David.

"I'm taking you both to the principal's office right now," William said. "Come on, let's go!"

David turned to go to the principal's office, and glanced into Mr. Morrison's room. He saw Carol, tears streaming down her cheeks and a terrified look on her face. She had seen the whole thing.

"How could he do such a thing?" Carol thought.

William sat in his room during second period, which was a free period, thinking about how David and Carol had both acted during homeroom and first period. It was so unlike them. Carol was always so cheerful. And David was not the type of person to get into a fight. He came up with an idea and decided to take a quick walk to Erica's classroom.

William knocked on the door and opened it. She had a class, but he had to tell her his idea.

"Are you doing anything important?" William asked, smiling.

"Not really," Erica said. "My students here didn't do their homework reading, so I'm making them do it now."

"How beautifully evil," William said, laughing. "Can you come out into the hall and talk for a minute?"

"Yes," Erica said. "I'll be watching you all, so don't try and stop reading while I'm in the hall."

They walked out into the hall, keeping her door open so she could watch her students.

William explained to her about how strange David and Carol had acted.

"I don't understand," William said. "I know it's not any of my business, but they're my best students and I have to know what is going one. I know me and it'll bug me if I don't, so here's what I'm thinking. During lunch, we have them both paged to my room. We can all sit down and discuss what is happening."

"If you think it's a good idea, than so do I," Erica said. "I'll see you at eleven thirty."

"Eleven thirty," William said. He leaned in for a quick kiss and then walked back to his room. He opened up his laptop and began typing new ideas for his book, which he had been writing for some time.

At eleven thirty, William went to the office and asked for David and Carol to be paged to his room. When he got back to his room, Erica was sitting in a chair which was pulled up to his desk. He pulled his desk chair around to the front and sat in front of two desks, Erica by his side. David and Carol walked into the room. They both looked confused.

"Hello David, Carol," William said. "Would you mind having a seat in the desks in front of us?"

Neither of them said a word, but they moved forward and sat at the desks.

"I know you must be wondering why we had you called here," William said. "The reason is what happened this morning. Neither of you were acting like yourselves. Now I know it's none of my business-"

"No," Carol said, cutting him off. "It's not."

"I, uh, we just want to help if we can," William said, looking at Erica and then back at David and Carol.

David looked away and Carol took a deep breath. Carol put her hand on David's, who looked toward her. They knew that they needed someone to talk to, so they decided to tell William and Erica everything.

Suddenly, it all came out. Together, they explained everything, the possibility of Carol being pregnant, why David had gotten so angry, everything.

"I see," William said. "Well I hope that everything turns out alright, but perhaps next time you have, uh, an interaction of that sort, you should both be more careful."

"Yes," Erica said. "Love can make a lot of good things happen, but being stupid can make bad things happen. Like you two, you're the cutest couple I've ever seen and yet, you're fighting. And over something that you two should be together on, no matter how it turns out. It's both of your problem, not just Carol's, and definitely not just David's."

"I'm sorry," David said, looking at Carol. "For everything. I know that I scared you this morning. I was only thinking of myself and we need to be together on this. It was just such a shock. Of all the things that I was expecting, of all the things I thought were wrong, that never even crossed my mind."

"It's okay," Carol said. "I forgive you."

They hugged and William and Erica smiled. They knew that they had done something good. They had saved a relationship.

"You two had better get to class," William said, looking at the clock. "I'll see you tomorrow morning."

David and Carol said goodbye and walked out of the room.

"We just did a very good thing," William said, still smiling.

"Yes we did," Erica said. "It reminds me of high school, makes me feel young."

"Maybe tonight we will both feel young," William said, chuckling. He kissed Erica and she walked out of the room, winking at William before walking across the hall to her classroom.

David got home from school and went to his room. He threw his backpack across the room and lay down in his bed to take a nap. The phone rang and he got up to go get it. It was Carol.

"Hi," Carol said.

"Hi," David said.

"I'm not pregnant," Carol said.

"That's great," David said. "Not that it would have been an entirely bad thing if you were, just-"

"At our age, it would've, there's no denying that," Carol said, relief in her voice.

"Either way," David said. "I think that we should slow our relationship down. We don't need sex to be happy."

"Yeah," Carol said, unenthusiastically. "Look, David, I don't want to upset you, but you really did scare me today. You have always been a very happy go lucky person, not angry at all, but it's not something that I can just forget. I'm scared that you might get into more fights or even hurt me."

"Carol," David said. "I would never hurt you, trust me."

"I thought I could," Carol said. "I'm sorry, but I think we should break up, at least for now. Bye."

Carol hung up and David stood there, tears streaming down his face. He didn't know what to do. He loved Carol more than anything in the world. He went into his room and lay down on his bed. He had to figure out a way to get her back, but how? He toyed with multiple ideas, but they all seemed so generic. He thought that maybe if he acted like himself and showed her that he wasn't a violent person, that she would take her back. He wasn't sure that his idea would work, so he closed his eyes and fell asleep, trying to find a better way to make it all better.

CHAPTER 7

November seemed to go on forever for David and Carol. Despite the fact that they had homeroom and English together, they barely ever spoke to one another. Their breakup had taken a toll on their friendship that they hadn't wanted.

They had wanted their friendship to grow more even though they weren't dating, but it wasn't happening. David had made a few attempts to talk to Carol on his own with limited success.

She ignored him for the most part and when she did talk to him it was to tell him to stop talking to her. It hurt David because she was the only girl he had ever really liked, nonetheless gotten close to.

David was still trying to figure out exactly what had happened. He had written Carol several notes, trying to explain to her that the fight he had gotten into was out of anger, an emotion which he didn't show that often.

November went surprisingly well, however, for William and Erica. They were extremely happy living together. They had finally settled into a routine of getting up together in the morning, watching the news and finally eating breakfast together, all before going to work.

They had managed their schedules so that they could have lunch together every day, switching between each others' rooms day by day. In order to keep the lunch work related, they only talked about their classes and students. They saved their personal affairs for when they got home around 3:30 each afternoon.

They had dinner every night around 5:00 and went to bed at 10:00. They tried to do something new and exciting every weekend.

One weekend, they had both decided to try skydiving, which had seemed like a fantastic idea at the time. They had arrived at the airport at nine o'clock in the morning, which was their first mistake. They did eat breakfast in the morning, but the problem was that both of them had developed a habit for consuming more coffee than food in their morning. That was their second mistake.

Their third mistake seemed to be the fact that they finally both gave in and got into the airplane. Once they were in the air, they both knew that they had made a huge mistake, but they both had too much pride to turn it down now.

A half hour later, after enjoying the scenery from above, they jumped. They didn't do much of a countdown, because at that point they just wanted to get it over with.

After they jumped, they were in the air for fifteen seconds before they both pulled their parachute cords. They pulled them earlier than they had been told to.

The combination of the pain from the cords and the coffee breakfast made William throw up immediately. He watched as his vomit fell to the ground, wondering if it hit anyone. The thought made him chuckle.

Erica made herself over to him and they held hands the rest of the way down. Once they hit ground, they both vomited. After a short, yet much needed nap in the airport, they both got into the car, where they vowed to never do that ever again as long as they should both live.

Nevertheless, life was great for them. They had it all, which really only amounted to each other, but that was fine with them.

William was finally finished with his book and was currently looking around for publishers. Erica had edited it herself and William had asked another friend look at it just for another opinion.

He wanted to get it published soon because he wanted money to buy Erica a ring. They had been together long enough in his opinion and they were deeply in love. It seemed to William like fate had brought them together seeing as how they had gone to the same high school although they had never crossed paths.

He had made the executive decision to ask Erica to be his wife. The only problem was he had no idea how to do it. He thought about asking his father, but in their old age, his parents had started telling each other everything so that was no good. He knew that his mother would never be able to keep her mouth shut, and one way or another, it would make its way back to Erica before the right time.

Robert crossed his mind, but Robert knew about getting women in bed, not about getting them to marry him.

After giving it some thought, he decided to set up a meeting with Mrs. Jodi King, the principle of Bucksport High and William's boss. She had been married to her husband for thirty years, so William was sure that she knew a thing or two about the subject. He decided to go to her office before classes started the next morning and talk to her.

"Jodi, can I speak with you for a minute," William asked after walking into her office.

"Of course, William," Jodi said, gesturing him toward a chair.

William sat down and began to explain his situation.

"I really love Erica," William said. "I want to ask her to marry me but we've only been together for a few months. Do you think it's too soon?"

"It really depends," Jodi said. "Does it feel like it's too soon?"

"I don't know," William said, chuckling. "I feel like one of my students, talking to you like this."

"I'm pretty sure that marriage is a more serious issue than any that a high school student would face," Jodi said, smiling.

"I suppose you're right," William said. "I just don't know what to do."

"Well, William," Jodi said. "It's a very personal issue, but if it feels right to you, I'm sure that it will feel right to Erica. The only thing you're afraid of is rejection, which is normal. That's why you're here, getting a second opinion. You think that if you ask, she'll say 'no'. It's very cliché, but if it's meant to be, then it will all work out."

"Alright, Jodi," William said. "Thank you very much."

William stood up and walked out of Jodi's office, walking up to his room. Homeroom was the same as always, the same boring attendance taking and then sitting there watching students, sipping coffee while he tried not to fall asleep.

There were rarely any changes in his daily routine, but when there were, he held onto those moments as long as he could. It seemed like the only times in his day that weren't boring were lunch and after school when he got to spend time with Erica. Even when they were both working at home, just being together was enough to make the time go by smoothly.

William observed that the relationship between David and Carol had not approved and that although David tried talking to her, Carol seemed to ignore him. He thought this was too bad because they had seemed so perfect for each other. He pondered why Carol had taken it so badly when David had gotten in one measly fight. It *had* been a stressful situation. I mean, he had just found out that his girlfriend may be pregnant.

His thoughts were interrupted as the bell rang and he stood up to begin teaching his first period class.

Before William and Erica knew, the day was over and they walked outside to William's car and rode home. William seemed distant to Erica, which was never the case with him.

He was pondering what Jodi had said that morning.

"Erica, do you love me?" William suddenly asked.

"Of course I love you," Erica said, shocked at the question.

"Yeah, I know," William said. "But I mean, do you *really* love me?"

"William," Erica said, taking his hand. "I wouldn't want to be with anyone else but you."

William smiled and immediately began preparing his proposal.

David had become very depressed. It was bad enough that Carol had broken up with him, but the fact that she wouldn't even speak to him made it much worse. Not a day went by when he didn't think about the time that the two of them had spent together.

What did I do? He would think to himself over and over. *All I did was show my emotion. Don't girls usually complain when guys* don't *show their emotions?*

The thought made him momentarily crack a smile, but then he was back to being depressed again.

He thought about calling Carol, but he figured that it would be pointless and that she would just hang up. He wanted to make everything up to her but he didn't know how. There wasn't much to do in such a small town.

"Stupid small town," David said, falling back onto his bed. "Why did she have to break up with me?"

David knew that spending money on Carol wouldn't bring her back, but how else was he going to get her back? He had to think of something. Thanksgiving break was coming up and he decided to wait until afterward to try to get her back.

Thanksgiving was William's favorite holiday, and having Erica made it even better. They invited their parents' to eat with them and they had an amazing dinner. Both Erica and William's mother's cooked a turkey and a cavalcade of pies that would have fed a dinner at the White House.

They sat down, surrounding two large tables that Kathleen and Mona had taped together to look like one large one, which left way too much extra space, but William didn't want to say anything.

After a hectic five minutes of passing potatoes, stuffing, pieces of turkey and other various vegetables, they had finally all filled their plates and were ready to eat.

"This looks so good," William said before taking his first bite. "Thank you for cooking it."

Kathleen and Mona both said thank you and then began eating the food themselves.

"I want to say something," Carl said. "And it's going to be really sappy, so just bare with me."

Everyone smiled and gave Carl their full attention.

"Three months ago," Carl began. "Erica was not happy. She wouldn't tell anyone this, but it was true. And the only reason I bring it up at all is this. Three months ago, I also received a phone call from my little girl, telling me about a wonderful guy she had met named William. I was excited to meet this 'William', the person who was making my daughter so happy.

"When I met him, he didn't disappoint me. He was just as wonderful as she had described to me. And his family was just as wonderful. I just want to thank you, William and your dear parents for being so kind and for welcoming not only my daughter, who I know you love *very* much, but also welcoming my wife and I into your family."

As he finished, he winked at William, almost as to hint that he could feel that William was planning to propose.

"That was a beautiful speech," William said, raising his glass. "To parents, old and new, and to a lifelong family."

They all raised their glasses. They made small talk for the remainder of the meal.

"What an amazing dinner," said Stephen when they had finished their desert.

"I won't argue with that, Stephen," Carl said. "Your wife knows how to cook a pie."

They chuckled and then Erica and William's parents' left.

Erica and William cleaned up the table and then they went into their bedroom. William took off his shirt and pants. He leaned in and his lips touched Erica's. They laid down on their bed and William moaned as he moved forward.

It was the first day back after Thanksgiving break and David had made the decision to give Carol one last chance. He walked up to her in homeroom and sat down next to her.

"Carol," David said. "Not being with you hurts more than you could ever know. Will you come to the park with me after school and talk about us?"

For the first time since they broke up, Carol looked up at David. She smiled and hugged David.

"I've missed you too," Carol said, her eyes tearing up. "I'd love to go to the park after school and talk."

"Alright," David said. "I'll meet you by the lobby."

After school, David went to the lobby where Carol was waiting. They didn't say anything on the walk to the park. They sat down on the swings and each tried to talk at the same time.

"You go first," David said, taking Carol's hand.

"David, I want to be there through the good and the bad times," Carol said. "I broke up with you when I needed you the most. I guess the whole pregnancy thing freaked me out."

"You and me both," David said, letting out half a laugh. "It really hurt me when you wouldn't even talk to me."

"I'm sorry David," Carol said. "I didn't ever mean to hurt you. It was just, I thought I was pregnant and then, you punched someone instead of talking to me. You shut me out and *that* hurt me. I need you, David. You're the only one that I can talk to. I love you, David."

"I love you too Carol," David said. "But let's take it slow this time."

"That sounds like a great idea," Carol said, laughing. "In fact, let's start over completely. I'm Carol."

"I'm David," said David. "Would you like to go to the movies with me this weekend, Carol?"

"I'd love to," Carol said. They fell into each others arms and stayed there for an hour. Then David walked Carol home.

David was happier than he had been for a long time. Carol said she was too but it was still going to take some adjusting. Before they knew it, December break was upon them and they were out of school again. They began spending nights at each others houses like they had before. This time, however, one would sleep in the bed and one on the couch to ensure that nothing happened. They found very quickly that they were actually happier without physical love.

Christmas Eve, they got together and exchanged gifts and then as a gift to each other, they slept in the same bed. They didn't have sex, but they cuddled all night. It was very sensual and felt better than if they *had* had sex.

Christmas Eve was also a very special night at William and Erica's house. They exchanged all of their presents and they kissed. Then William stood up and said he was going to the bedroom real quick.

He got into the bedroom and pulled open his underwear drawer. He pulled out the ring case and slipped it into his pocket. He felt like he was going to throw up so he ran to the bathroom. He didn't throw up, but he splashed some water on his face and looked into the mirror.

"You can do this," William said to himself. "You don't want anything more than this right now. Not even that wonderful sweater that Erica bought you."

He nervously laughed at his last line and shut off the bathroom light. Then he walked back out into the living room.

When he got there, he reached into his pocket and got down on one knee.

"Erica Young," William started. "We've only known each other since September, but I guarantee I will never find anyone like you. I know that you are the one who I want to spend the rest of my life with."

Tears of joy were streaming down Erica's face as William pulled out the ring and took her hand in hers.

"Erica," William said. "Will you marry me?"

"Yes," Erica yelled. "Yes, William I will!"

She embraced him, squeezing harder than she ever had. Erica could hardly believe what was happening, but then again neither could William. Never in his wildest dreams had he ever thought he would meet anyone as Erica Young and now he was her fiancé. It was literately a dream come true.

Tears of joy were streaming down his face as well. He pulled back from the embrace and kissed Erica with more passion than he had ever felt. They laid down on the couch together, where they soon fell asleep, smiling and staring at the beautiful Christmas Tree.

Even as William began to fall asleep, he couldn't believe what had just happened. His heart was beating even faster than before he had pulled out the ring. He could barely believe that he was engaged to marry the most beautiful girl he had ever met in his life. He pulled her closer as he envisioned the life they would lead together, their children, their grandchildren. His heart beat hard he fell into a very deep sleep.

Part Two

JANUARY TO JULY

CHAPTER 8

January was a very cold month, but David and Carol didn't notice. Their love was enough to keep each other warm enough. They had never been happier. Carol had expressed multiple times how happy she had been since David had asked her out again.

After they had decided to take it slow, they had sat down and had a long discussion about exactly what that meant. After some compromising, they had agreed that they would go no further than making out, no matter what they thought they wanted.

They went out to the movies nearly every weekend, sometimes watching one at Carol's house. One of their agreements had been that they would only go to Carol's house to hang out, and only when Alice was there to ensure that they didn't have sex. The final agreement was that if David were to spend the night at Carol's, he was to sleep on the couch in the living room.

Alice wasn't particularly happy that Carol had taken David back so suddenly after what Carol had told her happened, but she loved seeing her daughter happy, so she didn't say anything about it.

At school, David had become somewhat friends with William Morrison, after showing him one of his stories and William gave him some constructive criticism on how to make it better. Ever since then, they had often stayed after school and had conversations about writing and their favorite authors. On days when she didn't have much homework, Carol joined their conversations, and often times, Erica would join them as well.

William and Erica had invited David in Carol to attend the wedding, which was to be held in June. They had accepted the invitation with wide smiles. David had told William later that he couldn't think of a more romantic date than that of a wedding.

"Why are you so interested in the dark side of life?" William asked David one day after school.

Carol was sitting next to David, waiting intently for his answer. Erica had a slight cold and hadn't been able to make it to work that day.

"It's just more realistic," David said. "Not to say that fantasy isn't good to write about or read, but when you're done with those stories the worlds within are gone. At least with darker stories you start in the world you live in and you end there as well."

"Fascinating," William said. "I would agree that the stories are definitely more realistic, but sometimes I think we all need a trip away from reality. What do you think, Carol?"

"I disagree completely," Carol said, smiling. "I began writing when I was young so that I could create my own worlds and even creatures to get me away from the real world."

"See, David," William said. "I think most people definitely read and write for that reason. But that isn't to say that darker writing isn't important. You're a great writer and you should keep it up."

"Thank you very much, Mr. Morrison," said David. "You've been a great influence on me, and I'm not just saying that. I've never really shown my writing to anyone who took it seriously before."

"That's too bad," William said. "Because you can't improve your writing when people are all telling you you're a great writer, you need to be told where you could improve as well.." William looked at the clock. "We'd all better be going, it's nearly three thirty."

"Is it really?" David asked. "I swear that we could literately talk for hours and not even notice."

"Do you two need a ride home?" William asked, sliding his brown jacket over the sweater he was wearing.

"No," David said. "We can walk."

"It's such a nice day," Carol said, looking out the window.

"That's true," William said. "I almost wish I could walk home, but I live too far away for that." He laughed and they all walked out of his classroom.

The three of them walked out to the parking lot, where William got into his car. He rolled down the window and said goodbye to David and Carol. David and Carol said goodbye and they began walking to Carol's house.

It was a Friday and they had decided to do homework at Carol's and then stay up late and watch some movies in the living room.

When they got to Carol's house they walked into the living room. They took out their notebooks and they started doing homework. David was working on math homework and Carol was studying for a Biology test she had coming up the following week.

Alice wasn't home yet, and wouldn't be for a couple of hours. That made Carol uneasy because she was afraid of what Alice would think when she returned home. She knew that Alice hadn't really been too happy about her getting back together with David.

David was uneasy as well, but not for the same reason. Without Alice there, David was beginning to feel urges. He always felt these urges when he was at Carol's, but when Alice was there, he was able to keep them at bay. But now, they were alone, and they were sitting on a couch, right next to each other. It wouldn't take any time at all to get undressed and have a quickie.

David knew that they had agreed against it, so he tried to take his mind off of it by doing his math homework. But try as he might, he couldn't get his mind off of it. He began to get antsy in his seat, moving his legs around and moving around. Finally he stood up.

"I'll be right back," David said. "I've got to go to the bathroom."

"Okay," Carol said, not even looking up from her Biology book.

David quickly walked out of the room and into the bathroom. He stared at himself in the mirror.

"*What am I doing?*" David thought. "*We're not going to have sex, so just stop thinking about it.*"

David thought over and over about what had happened before and how it could easily happen again.

"*What are the chances that it would happen twice?*" David thought, toying with the idea. "*Maybe I should just go home. I'll tell Carol I don't feel good or something.*"

David thought about it for a few more minutes and then he walked out of the bathroom and back into the living room. Without saying anything, he sat back down on the couch and picked up his math homework again.

David looked over at Carol, who returned the look. David smiled and leaned in and kissed her.

"David," Carol said. "I think we should work on homework."

"I know," David said. "But I just want to kiss you for a few minutes. It won't lead to anything, I swear."

"Alright," said Carol, putting down her Biology book.

David moved in closer and started kissing Carol. They laid down on the couch and began making out. Before they knew it, their shirts were off. Carol knew they had said that they wouldn't have sex but she didn't care.

As David began slipping off Carol's pants, the front door opened and Alice walked in.

David and Carol both froze, not knowing what to do.

"Carol," yelled Alice as she walked into the living room. "*What* is going on?"

"I, uh," Carol stammered.

"David," Alice said sternly. "I think you should go home."

David didn't say a word. He just stood up and put on his shirt. He quickly grabbed his backpack and ran out the front door. Alice started laughing uncontrollably.

"Why are you laughing? I thought you were mad," Carol said, confused.

"Oh," Alice said. "I'm furious, but the situation is pretty funny."

After laughing for a couple more minutes, Alice looked at Carol.

"You're not grounded. I can't help your stupid mistakes," Alice said. "But I don't want David to come over for a week. You can see him at school, you can even go for walks with him, but I don't want him in this house. Understood?"

"Yes," Carol said.

She stood up and got her Biology book and went to her room. When Carol got to her room she happened to see herself in her mirror. Her face was bright red and for a second it made her smile.

Then she got a mortified look on her face. Not only had her and David broken their promise to each other, Alice had walked in. It all hit her all at once and she lied down on her bed and closed her eyes, tears rolling down her cheeks. She fell asleep, playing the events which had just happened over and over in her head.

David walked home quite slowly. He wanted to laugh, but he wanted to cry at the same time. Why had he done that? What would he tell Brenda? It was all so awful he wished he could just do it all over, but he couldn't. He decided that he would call Carol after supper and see if she wanted to go for a quick walk.

He got home and told Brenda that he wasn't feeling well. Then he walked into his room and finished his math homework.

On the way home, William had stopped at a flower shop and picked up a bouquet of roses for Erica. He pulled into the driveway and got out of his car. When he got inside, he walked into their bedroom where Erica was on their bed reading.

"Hello," Erica said. "You're home a bit late."

"Yeah, sorry," William said. "David and Carol came in and we talked for a little bit longer than we anticipated."

"What's behind your back?" Erica asked, smiling.

"Something for you," William said, pulling out the roses and taking them over to her.

"Their beautiful, William," Erica said, smelling them. "Thank you so much."

Erica leaned up and kissed William on the cheek.

"Are you feeling better?" William asked.

"Yes," Erica said. "I think I just caught a small cold."

"How about I order Chinese tonight and we just take it slow this evening?" William suggested.

"That," Erica said. "Sounds like a fantastic idea."

William smiled and climbed into bed with Erica, kissing her as soon as he lied down.

The phone rang about an hour after they had finished, and William danced his way to the kitchen and answered it.

"Hey Robert," William said. "Tonight? I don't know, man, I've got work tomorrow, not sure if a bar's a good idea. Hey, wait a minute-"

William held the phone to his chest so that Robert couldn't hear him.

"Honey," William said. "What's your sister doing tonight?"

"I don't know," Erica said. "Why?"

"Robert wants to go out to a bar, but that's not going to happen. What if we go get Lilly and make it a double date?"

Erica smiled. "I bet Lilly would go for that," She said. "How about Robert?"

"Hold on," William said. "Hey, Robert, how about going on a date tonight? With Lilly, Erica's sister. Alright, we'll call her and set it up. Meet us at Eastman's? Okay, see you there."

Erica walked into the kitchen, took the phone from William and dialed Lilly's number.

After what felt to William like an hour long conversation, Erica hung up the phone and they were in the car. They drove to the other side of town and picked up Lilly. Then they drove back across town to Eastman's.

They met Robert outside and the four of them walked in together. They were seated and ordered a bottle of red wine for the table.

"So, Lilly," Robert said, nervously. "I haven't seen you since the party."

"I know," Lilly said. "I've been busy with work and everything."

"I think we all have," William said. "It seems like it's all there is to do lately."

They all went silent for a couple of seconds, until Erica broke the silence.

"So, Lilly," she said. "The last time I talked to you you were up for a promotion. How did that go?"

"I got it," Lilly exclaimed. "I can't believe I forgot to tell you! I have an office with a *window* now!"

Lilly laughed out loud.

"That's great," Erica said. "I'm so happy for you."

"What do you do," Robert said, taking a sip of wine.

"I'm an attorney," Lilly said.

"Fascinating," Robert said. "The closest I ever came to that is being a fan of crime dramas."

"You know, Robert," William said, chuckling. "I recall the last time I talked to you as well. I believe you were trying to figure out what kind of beer to drink that night."

"Shut up," Robert said, smiling. He looked at Lilly. "He's probably right, but I *do* have a job. I drive trucks for Wal-Mart."

"Well that's interesting too," Lilly said.

The waiter came over and took all of their orders.

"And bring another bottle of wine," Robert said, half joking.

"So," William said. "Speaking of your job, how's it going?"

"It's going well," Robert said. "It has the same perks as always. I get to drive for a living. I think it's one of the most enjoyable jobs that anyone could have. You're literately payed for traveling, and that's it."

"I love traveling," Lilly said. "But I don't get to do much traveling anymore, not the way I'd like to anyway. You have it made. Like you said, it's like you're payed to go on road trips."

"You know," Robert said, smiling at Lilly, "Another perk of my job is that I'm allowed to take anyone I want with me."

"Really," Lilly said.

"Well," Robert said. "It's not in the rule book, but I'll put it this way: my boss wouldn't fault me for it."

Lilly turned a bit red and quickly turned away.

The waiter got to the table with their food and began putting it in front of them.

"Look at that service," Lilly said. "I've never got food that quick at a restaurant before."

"We all ordered sandwiches," Erica said, confused. "Of course the service was quick."

Lilly shot her back a look and mouthed "duh". Erica burst out laughing.

Lilly, still embarrassed, quickly picked up her sandwich and bit into it.

"That smells great," Robert said. "What is it?"

"Ham and cheese with cranberry mayo," Lilly said. "My coworkers say it's stiff and boring because I get it every day."

"I don't think it's stiff *or* boring," Robert said. "I think it's kind of...wild and crazy. And that smell, it's kind of...sexy."

Lilly took another bite and chewed slowly, almost as though she didn't want to swallow because she wasn't sure what to say to that last comment. She swallowed and managed a weak "thank you".

"You've got a bit of mayo on your lip," Robert said, reaching over and wiping it off with his index finger. He put the finger in his mouth and tasted the cranberry mayo.

"Delicious," Robert said. "I'll have to have this sometime."

Erica looked at her watch.

"Well," Erica said. "I didn't realize how late it was getting. William and I have to head out. Sir, can we get these to go."

"But it's only-" William started.

Erica shot him a look that said "shut up".

The waiter got them boxes and they both stood up.

"Goodbye," Erica said to Lilly, hugging her.

"Bye, man," William said to Robert.

Once in the car, William looked at Erica.

"So why did we leave so early?" He asked.

"Because," Erica said. "They were really hitting it off. I think we just did something really good."

"Well," William said. "Since it is still early, how about you and I go back home and have some cranberry mayo of our own?"

Erica leaned in and kissed him on the lips.

"Delicious," she said.

William put his key in the ignition and drove back across town to their house.

David called Carol's house at six o'clock and was very thankful that Carol picked up the phone. David was glad to hear her voice, but he could hear a certain sadness.

"What's wrong?" David asked.

"You can't come over to my house for a week," Carol said. "And I can't go over to yours."

"Oh," David said. "Can we still go on walks?"

"Yes," Carol said. "I can see you outside of school, just not at either of our houses."

"Oh," David said. "Would you like to go for a walk now?"

"Yes," Carol said happily. "I'll meet you half way."

David walked outside, a large smile on his face, and began walking toward Carol's house. He laughed to himself, thinking about Alice's face. He was sure that his was quite a site as well.

Then he wondered how he would be able to look at her again. The thought was a bit scary, but it also made him laugh. He saw Carol up ahead and waved to her.

"Hey," David said. "How are you?"

"I'm good," Carol said. "Look, I want this to work out, I really do. Not a moment goes by that I wish we had never had sex in the first place. It seems to have made things so complicated."

"I know what you mean," David said. "I remember reading once how sex is supposed to bring people closer, which may be true, but I'm with you. If we hadn't ever done it, we wouldn't be as tempted to do it every time we see one another." His face seemed to fill with sadness.

"I'm not mad, David," Carol said, shaking her head. "I was simply making an observation." She smiled.

"I guess that some *would* say that it's only natural given our ages," David said.

David and Carol walked to the park and sat down on a bench. They leaned into one another and just sat there, breathing in the fresh air. They rested their eyes, but didn't fall asleep. They just sat there, enjoying their time together and the silence. After about an hour, they stood up and David kissed Carol. He walked her home and then he walked home himself.

CHAPTER 9

David hadn't taken the slightest liking to any other girl except for Carol since they had started dating. She was perfect for him as he was for her. By February, they had completely patched things up and had calmed their hormones enough so that they were able to spend days at a time together without even thinking about sex. Everything seemed to be going well for them until one day when David received an unexpected invitation.

Jeffery Bedford was the captain of the Football team. His hair was blonde and short. His eyes were bright blue, every girl's fantasy. He was the equivalent of a group of kids trying to pressure another into something, good or bad. What he said went at Buckspot High School.

David was walking down the hall, when it happened. Jeffery stopped him in the hallway and handed him an envelope.

"What's this?" David said.

"It's an invitation to my birthday party this Friday night, David," Jeffery said. "Only guys allowed."

"You-You know my name?" David asked.

"Of course," Jeffery said. "If you go to this school, I know you. Be there or else, buddy." Jeffery chuckled at his 'joke' as he walked away.

"*Wow*," David thought. "*I get to go to Jeffery's party. What will I wear? Should I buy him a gift?*" These questions and others circled through his mind. He walked off, still in awe of what had happened.

After school, David told Carol what had happened.

"That's cool," Carol said. "You should go."

"Really," David asked.

"Yeah," Carol said. "Maybe you'll meet some new friends. That would be cool."

Friday came quick and at seven o'clock, David walked half a mile to the 'good' part of town, where the more wealthy families lived. He knocked on the door of Jeffery's house and waited. He could hear loud music and laughing through the door. The door opened and Jeffery stood there.

"David," Jeffery said. "I'm so glad you could make it, come on in."

David was very nervous because he didn't even know Jeffery and yet he was acting as though they had been friends for years. As nervous as he was, he was equally excited to be in the house of the most popular person at school.

"I got you a present," David said.

"Set it over there," Jeffery said, pointing to a large table that looked like that at an infant's birthday. The amount of presents was overwhelming. David set his present down and headed in the direction of the music and laughing.

Jeffery was nowhere in sight and David didn't know any of the other people at the party. He recognized one guy from his Math class, but he had never talked to him before.

David found the living room and sat down on the couch. Jeffery came in and handed David a cup.

"What are you doing in here all alone?" Jeffery asked.

"I don't know anyone here," David said. "I don't even really know you that well."

"I know," Jeffery said. "You're probably wondering why I asked you to come, aren't you?"

"Yeah I am," David laughed, sipping the drink. David coughed. "What's in this?"

"It's beer," Jeffery said. "Haven't you ever had any?"

"Of course," David lied. "Plenty of times."

"You're lying," Jeffery said, laughing loudly. "It's okay, I won't judge. I asked you to come, by the way, because I found one of your stories in the printer. Nobody knows this, but I'm a writer also. I really liked your story and I wanted to know if you wanted to hang out sometime."

"Really," David exclaimed, completely ignoring the fact that Jeffery had stolen one of his stories and hadn't returned it. "You're a writer?"

"Yeah," Jeffery said. "But don't tell anyone. No offense, but my friends wouldn't think it was very cool. You can leave if you want, but you should stick around. I think you will have a good time." Jeffery smiled and stood up, walking into the kitchen.

Something wasn't right in how Jeffery said that last sentence, but David shrugged it off. He took another sip. He was getting used to the awful taste quickly. He finished off his cup and went to the kitchen to get some more.

By the time the girls showed up, David was too buzzed to remember that Jeffery had told him that there would only be guys at the party. He even forgot about Carol, as a skinny blonde girl began walking toward him.

"Hey," said the girl. "What's your name?"

"My name's David," David said, leaning up against the wall trying to look cool.

"I'm Alyssa," said the girl. "You're cute."

"Really, you think so," David slurred. "You're not too bad yourself." He winked and took a step forward, falling flat on his face.

Alyssa helped him up and she giggled. Then she pulled him close and started kissing him. He wrapped his arms around her and used her as means to keep from falling down. He kissed her back and soon, they were searching for a bedroom.

They found one and before the door was even closed, both of their shirts were off and on the floor. Alyssa closed the door and pulled off her pants. David pulled off his pants as well, and then they hit the bed, making out more passionately than before. Alyssa, who was on bottom, wrapped her legs around David.

They rolled to their sides and David reached for her back. After a slight struggle, he pulled off her bra and threw it to the floor. She flipped him onto his back and pulled off his boxers and her panties. She kissed him once more and slowly slid onto him.

Saturday morning, David's head felt like someone had run it over with a bus. It took him a minute for his blurry vision to leave. He wasn't sure where he was, but he knew that he was naked. He turned his head and saw Alyssa, lying there naked.

What the hell did I do, David thought. He jumped out of bed and put on his clothes.

He tried running toward the door but fell down in the process. He opened the door and slowly made his way to the front door and left. He slowly walked back to his house, his headache only getting worse.

How could he do such a thing? How would he be able to face Carol? He made it back to his house and walked inside.

"You could have told me that you were going to be staying the night," Brenda snapped. "I was up all night."

"Sorry Brenda," David said, slowly.

"Are you *drunk*?" Brenda asked.

"No," David said. "I'm fine." With that, he suddenly threw up on the kitchen floor.

William woke up Saturday morning to the sound of the phone ringing.

"Go get that," Erica said, still half asleep.

William stood up and walked out into the kitchen and picked up the phone. It was Robert.

"Hey, man," Robert said.

"Hey," William said drowsily. "Why are you calling me at-" William looked at the clock, "eight o'clock in the morning?"

"I'm having a party tonight," Robert said. "I'm sorry it's late notice, but the whole thing just kind of got thrown together. Can you make it? You can bring Erica with you if you want."

"I'll ask her when she gets up," William said. "Then I'll call you back."

William hung up the phone and walked back to his bedroom where he fell asleep for another hour.

William and Erica woke up and went out to the kitchen, where Erica began making coffee.

"So who called this morning?" Erica asked.

William had to think for a minute before he remembered that Robert had called.

"It was Robert," William said. "He said he's having a party tonight that he wants us to come to."

"You can go if you want," Erica said. "I have a lot of papers to grade."

"Are you sure?" William asked.

"Yeah," Erica said. "You haven't hung out with Robert on your own for a while. You'll probably have a good time." She smiled at him and brought him over a cup of coffee.

William drank about half of his coffee, enough to be coherent, and then he walked over to the phone and called Robert.

The party was at seven, and William left the house at six, so that he could have a few minutes to talk to Robert and catch up before the party started. He pulled into Robert's driveway and reached over to the passenger's seat where he had a 24 pack of beer that he had bought at the store. He carried the beer up to Roberts door and knocked. Robert came over, a beer already in his hand, and let him in.

"I'm really glad you could make it, man," Robert said. "It's too bad that Erica said, but I understand about having work."

"Yeah," William said. "We've both kind of been putting work off to the last minute lately."

"You ol' dog," Robert said, laughing.

William laughed too and they walked into the kitchen and put William's beer in the fridge, but not before he grabbed one for himself. They sat down at the kitchen table and waited for the other guests to arrive.

There weren't that many people at the party, maybe ten. William talked to Robert mostly.

"Where's Lilly tonight," William asked.

"Same as Erica," Robert said. "She's busy with work tonight and couldn't make it."

"I see," William said. "I'll be right back, I'm going to get another beer."

He stood up from the couch in the living room and walked into the kitchen. That's when he saw her.

She was the most beautiful girl he had ever seen besides Erica. She had long, dirty blonde and curly hair. She was wearing skin tight leather jeans and a white tee shirt. William got a beer from the refrigerator.

"Hi," she said when William turned around.

"Hey," William said, opening the beer and taking a sip.

"I'm Julie," said the girl.

"I'm William," he said.

"William Morrison," Julie asked.

"Yes," William said, confused.

"I knew you looked familiar," Julie said.

"Julie White!" William exclaimed. "Now I remember. Wow, I haven't seen you since college."

"Yeah," Julie said, quietly.

William had dated Julie for three months but they had broken up shortly after William graduated. They had tried to continue dating, but it didn't work with the distance.

"So," William said. "How have you been?"

"I've been pretty good," Julie said. "I'm writing a book."

"That's cool," William said. "I'll keep an eye out."

"I still love you," Julie blurted. She turned red as a stop sign as soon as she said it.

"Julie," William said, his smile fading. "You can't be serious. That was so long ago, I mean I moved on, I'm engaged!"

"Well," Julie said. "She's very lucky."

"I like to think of me as the lucky one, I mean she's just—"

Julie was kissing him before he had a chance to finish his sentence. He was so shocked that it took him a few seconds to register what was happening. He shoved her back.

"Julie," William said. "I can't do this."

She leaned in again, and this time he let the kiss last a little over a minute before he shoved her back once again. He didn't speak another word, he just walked toward the door and left Robert's house.

He had made his way, quite quickly, back to his car and was driving. His heart was racing harder now than it ever had in his life. He didn't' know where to drive. Back home? No, not until he figured this all out.

What the hell had he done? Erica wasn't just his girlfriend, she was his fiancé and he loved her. He decided to drive to an abandoned park in the next town to park and figure everything out before he drove back home where he would have to confront Erica.

An hour later, he finally pulled into his driveway at 10:30. He slowly walked inside and into his bedroom, where Erica was still grading papers.

"Erica," William said nervously. "I have something I have to tell you."

"Okay," Erica said, putting down the paper she was grading.

"I ran into an old friend at the party," William said. "No, that's a lie. She was an old girlfriend. We got talking, and, well—"

"Well what," Erica said, a look of anger and concern appearing on her face.

"We kind of kissed for thirty seconds," William said, ashamed.

To his surprise, Erica began chuckling, despite the angry look on her face. Then she began smiling and laughing uncontrollably.

"Why are you laughing?" William asked.

"You *kissed* her?" Erica laughed. "Jeez the way you were acting I thought you had cheated on me."

"You're not mad?" William asked, confused.

"I'm not exactly happy," Erica said, still laughing. "But I think we can work through it."

William suppressed a smile and let out a small laugh, thinking of how he had sat in the car for an hour trying to think of some way to tell Erica so that she wouldn't be mad.

Erica put away the school work for the evening and leaned in for a kiss. Then they both cuddled up together and shut off the lights.

When David walked into school on Monday, everyone started to cheer, some yelling his name, some just yelling. David smiled at first, but then frowned. His sadness soon turned to anger as he not only realized why they were cheering, but also saw Carol walking toward him, tears streaming down her face.

Before he had time to say anything at all, he felt her right palm hit the left side of his face. His head jerked to the side on impact and tears filled his eyes. He looked up, seeing a blurry Carol, and opened his mouth.

"Carol," David said.

"Don't," Carol said. "Just *don't*."

She turned and walked away. David didn't know what to do, but he couldn't take a day of classes, so he turned, and reluctantly walked out the school's front door. He sneaked out back and walked up to the football field. He crawled under some bleachers and he closed his eyes. He tried to fall asleep but he couldn't.

The emptiness that he was feeling engulfed his body. He began to shake as he turned to his side. Before he knew it, he was weeping, out loud so that anyone could had heard it had they been near the football field. But he didn't care about that, as embarrassing as that would be. He deserved it.

The pain he had caused Carol was nothing compared to what he felt. He knew that no matter what he did, he could never get Carol back again. He didn't deserve her. She was so much better than him and he knew that now. He closed his eyes and was finally able to fall asleep to the sound of his guilt screaming in his ears.

CHAPTER 10

Erica woke up in a morning in late February, and ran into the bathroom. William hadn't woke up yet, but when he heard her vomiting, quite loudly, from the bathroom, he jumped out of bed and ran toward the bathroom.

"Erica," William said. "Are you okay?"

"What do you think," Erica managed to say, in between being sick.

"I meant do you think it's serious," William said.

Erica stopped and took a breath. "William," she yelled. "When is vomiting into a toilet not serious?"

William opened his mouth to once again explain what he had meant, but he stopped. She had been having terrible mood swings lately that neither one of them could explain.

He instead helped her up and walked her back into the room and picked up the phone. He called the school for her, to let them know that she wouldn't be into work today.

"Put down that phone," Erica said, taking a breath and a sip from her water bottle. "I'm fine, really."

The secretary had already answered and he told her that he had dialed the wrong number.

"Are you sure that you're alright?" William asked, a bit worried.

"Yeah," Erica said. "It's the strangest thing, but I feel fine now. Hey, would you mind me taking my car to work today?"

"Yeah, whatever you want," William said.

"I just want a bit of time to think," Erica said, smiling. "I'm gonna take a shower, I'll see you in a few minutes."

After her shower, Erica got dressed and poured herself some coffee in a travel mug. She left ten minutes before William, and headed downtown.

She pulled into the driveway of the pharmacy and parked her car. She got out of the car and walked inside. She couldn't believe what she was doing, and the thought made her chuckle to herself.

When she got to the aisle with the pregnancy tests, she began looking them over.

What's the difference, she thought, looking them all over. *They all say the same thing.*

She looked at her watch and saw that she only had ten minutes. She grabbed three different kinds and walked up to the counter. She quickly paid for them and walked back out into her car. Once in the car, she put the tests into her purse and turned the ignition. She drove to the school and, with her palms sweating, she walked to her classroom, where her homeroom students were already at their seats.

"Good morning," Erica said nervously. She sat down at her desk and took the lid off of her travel mug and took a large gulp of coffee.

Relax, she thought to herself. *You don't know yet. Keep calm until you do.*

All of her classes that morning were hell. She kept messing up what she was saying and giving the wrong directions.

At one point, a student asked if everything was alright and she said "yes", with a painted smile.

The lunch period began and she immediately stood up, heading for the door. She had intended on heading straight for the bathroom, but she was met at the door by William.

"Hey," he said. "How are you doing? I mean I don't mean to sound intrusive, but I was watching you all morning. You weren't exactly yourself. Is there something you want to talk about?"

"Later," Erica said. "I, uh, really have to pee."

She rushed passed him and practically ran to the girl's bathroom. She got into a stall and reached into her purse, pulling out the pharmacy bag and grabbing the first pregnancy test that her fingers touched.

She opened it up and read the directions. She grimaced, but she stood up and pulled down her pants. She urinated into the cup that came with the test. She set the cup on the back of the toilet and took out the dropper. She filled it about half way full and dropped it onto the test. The back of the box said that it could take up to ten minutes. She packed up her things and slowly walked out of the bathroom and luckily made it back to her room without being seen.

She opened up an empty drawer and put it in, keeping it slightly open. She then took a deep breath and realized that she hadn't washed her hands. She chuckled at herself and took out some hand sanitizer that she only used on rare occasions. She lathered her hands and let out a deep breath. She relaxed for a few minutes. Then, she took out an egg salad sandwich and began eating it.

She finished the sandwich and looked up at the clock. It had been ten minutes, and she carefully opened up the drawer and looked at the pregnancy test. It was blue.

David walked into his room when he got home from school and closed the door. He lay down on his bed and closed his eyes. He hadn't felt this low in a long time. He was a hundred percent sure that he had royally screwed things up this time. He hadn't just flirted with some girl at a party. He had cheated on his girlfriend. Brenda had tried to help, but he didn't care to have her help. It had been two weeks since it had all happened and Carol hadn't contacted him at all.

No calls, no walks, not even a "hey" in the hallway at school. Homeroom was the worst. David still sat in the back, as usual, but Carol now sat up front, as far away from him as she could get.

He had no idea what, if anything, he should do. He knew that any romance story or Lifetime original movie would tell him that it was all over, but he didn't want to believe that. He wanted to believe that there was at least a chance, but no matter how he thought about it, no matter how many times he turned it over and over in his head, he couldn't come up with a working solution. Finally, he decided to take up Brenda on her offer to help.

"Brenda," he said, walking out of his room into the kitchen, where she was cooking dinner. "Can we talk?"

"Of course we can," Brenda said. "But first, tell me, how are you doing? And give me an honest answer."

"I feel awful, like the lowest human being on the planet," David said.

"Good," Brenda said, to David's surprise. "You should."

"I thought you wanted to help me," David said, confused.

"I do," Brenda said. "But I just wanted to make sure that you could admit that what you did was terrible."

David nodded. "I really do love her, Brenda. I wish that I could take it all back, but I know that even if she dated me again, she could never forgive me for what I did."

"It sounds like you think it's all over," Brenda said.

"I don't know how it couldn't be," David said, looking at the floor. "That's the problem. I've thought of every possibility, but none of them seem to fix anything."

Brenda turned off the stove. She drained the spaghetti noodles. She mixed the meat sauce in and put some in two plates. She moved them to the table. She got each of them a glass of milk.

"Okay," Brenda said. "Let's talk."

David sat down at the table and took a small sip of milk.

"I've truly run out of ideas at this point," David said. "What advice do you have?"

"Well," Brenda said, trying to hold back her chuckling. "I don't think you're going to date her again. You cheated on her, David. There's nothing worse on a young girls' heart then being cheated on. *Especially* by her first boyfriend. The problems that will ensue, the trust issues alone, do you understand?"

"Yes," David said. "So, even if I can't get back together with her, do you think there's something I could do to at least make her feel better?"

"It would have to be pretty damn big, David," Brenda said. "And you'd better do it quick, whatever it is you can come up with."

David looked at the calender. It was Thursday, which meant that tomorrow there would be an assembly at school. He couldn't think of anything bigger, nothing that would make any sense anyway. He took a deep breath and finished his spaghetti in silence. He finished, put the plate in the sink and went into his room to begin writing his speech.

Erica had been quiet ever since her and William had gotten home. She glanced over every now and then, over the book she was reading, and smiled at William, but that was it. He had tried to talk to her several times but she didn't seem to be in the mood to talk.

It felt like it took days, but finally, it was time for dinner. They sat down at the table and began eating. William's concerned look told Erica that she had better say something soon.

"William," Erica said. "Have you ever thought about having children? I mean, I know we've never really discussed it before."

"Well," William said between bites. "I've always wanted a family, when I finally got settled down and had the financial security for it. Why do you ask?"

Erica tried to speak, but the words wouldn't vocalize. She looked around he room, at the wall, at the stove, anything to try to take her mind off of William's piercing, wondering eyes.

She picked up her glass of milk, took a long drink and took a deep breath.

"I'm pregnant," she exhaled.

William's eyes lit up. "Really?" he asked.

"You're really happy?" She replied.

"Well yeah," he said. "Aren't you?"

"I guess I still haven't fully processed it yet," Erica said, smiling. "William, we're going to have a baby."

William stood up and walked over to Erica. He took her hands and she stood up. Their lips met with a passion that they hadn't felt since their first kiss. They were going to have a family.

The kiss ended, and William looked down at the table. He saw the frozen dinners that they had lazily made and began laughing out loud.

"Let's go out somewhere to eat," William said. "To celebrate."

"It's already six thirty," Erica said. "And we have work in the morning."

"Frankly, my dear," William said, smiling. "I don't give a damn."

They both started laughing as they put away the food on the table. They got their coats and walked out to William's car.

It was an hour and a half until school started, and David was pacing back and forth in his room. He was smiling brightly. He took another sip of his coffee and stopped, in front of the mirror.

"Hello," David said, confidently. "I know that a lot of you know me because of something I did at a party recently..."

When he got to school, David immediately walked into principle Jodi King's office.

"Mrs. King?" David asked. "Can I talk to you?"

"Of course, David," Jodi said.

"I was wondering if it would be possible to speak at the assembly this afternoon," David said.

"I suppose that could be arranged," Jodi said. "But I need to know the reason."

"Well," David began. "As you may have heard, I made a really big mistake and ended up ruining my relationship with Carol Robinson. I know that the relationship's most likely finished, but I'd like to at least like a chance to explain myself."

Jodi took a deep breath. "I usually don't grant students time to talk about their personal lives at an assembly," she said. "But between you and me, I've heard the things that have been said about you, and I think it would be a good idea for you to 'explain' yourself."

"Thank you," David said, a bit embarrassed by the look she was giving him.

He left her office and walked to William's classroom. He sat down, in the back as usual, and pulled out his speech, going over it one last time before the school day started. The speech had been carefully written, and it made him proud. He smiled, reading the words carefully, looking for any mistakes. He didn't find any, and he put the paper back in his backpack.

William felt like the happiest man alive. He looked at his homeroom of students and just smiled. He didn't have any coffee, but he didn't need any. His excitement was more powerful than any caffeine. He closed his eyes and leaned back in his chair, remembering the amazing night that he had had with Erica.

They had gone to a diner downtown, called The Sunny Side Up. They pulled into the driveway and got out of the car. They walked inside and sat down. They hadn't stopped smiling, or holding each others hands since they had left the house.

They hadn't ordered anything special, just a couple of burgers with fries and a couple of Pepsi's

"Thank you," Ericca had said.

"For what?" William asked, taking a sip of Pepsi.

"For everything," Erica said. "I mean, my life didn't really even have a direction before I met you. It was stressful to say the least. Now I'm sitting here, engaged, and I'm going to have a family."

William put down his Pepsi, lifted her hand and kissed it.

"So," He said, smiling. "When are we going to tell the soon to be grandparents?"

"The who?" Erica asked.

"Our parents," William responded, laughing.

"Oh," Erica said, chuckling. "I don't know. Tomorrow?"

"Sounds like a plan," William said. "This is our night."

They finished up their meal and paid. Then they walked out to the car and drove back home, still smiling and holding each others' hands.

They got back home and went straight to their bedroom. Their clothes were practically off before they got through the doorway. Erica landed on the bed first, followed by William, who kissed her as soon as his skin touched hers, not missing a beat.

"I love you, Erica," William said.

Smiling, she said, "shut up," and pulled his head toward hers, kissing him.

He lifted her, placing her higher up on the bed, and slowly hovered over her. He slowly leaned down, kissing her neck. She moaned slightly as he thrust forward.

The bell rang and William was thrown out of his thoughts. His first class began to enter the classroom. He started to get up, but realized that he had an erection and he immediately sat back down.

He closed his eyes, chuckled to himself and took a sip of his coffee.

"We're going to spend class by giving you a chance to gain extra credit," William said. "Just write a short paper on anything you think of and pass it in at the end."

The assembly took place in the gymnasium and started at one o'clock and went until the end of the school day. David had been given permission to go first, so that he wouldn't interrupt what Jodi had called "important information."

"Hello," Jodi said. "Welcome to our monthly assembly. We'll get things under way shortly, but first, we have a student who would like to say a few words. David Craven, come on up."

The entire student body went quiet as David walked down to the podium that Jodi was standing at. They were clearly confused, wondering why David would want to give any kind of speech at an assembly.

David got to the Podium and Jodi walked over to the stage, where the other staff members were standing. David tried desperately to find someone in the bleachers to look at while he spoke, to help kill nerves, but he didn't find anyone. He realized that he was only wasting time and took a deep breath.

"H-hello," he stammered. "I know that a lot of you know me because of something I did at a party recently."

The crowd of rowdy teenagers erupted with accepting applause. One of the male student's actually yelled, "You go, David!"

David smiled weakly. "Well actually, that's why I'm here." He began slightly shaking and sweat was rolling off of his forehead.

"At that party, I did something awful." He swallowed hard. "I cheated on my girlfriend. Now, Carol, I want you to know that I am extremely sorry."

He didn't even realize that he was no longer reading from his speech that was in front of him. "I love you Carol," he said, tears beginning to run down his face."

Carol stood up, embarrassed, and walked down the bleachers. Then, she ran toward the door and left the room.

David heard someone in the bleachers say, "how pathetic," and one of the jocks yelled, "pussy!"

Jodi quickly walked over toward David and took his shoulder, moving him away from the podium.

"David, you're excused early," she said. "Go on home. You tried your best."

David could see from her face that she was only being nice and that she, like the people in the audience, thought that his attempt was pathetic. He turned and walked toward the same door that Carol had walked out of.

David began walking down the hallway toward the lobby, when he heard someone crying. He walked further and stopped in front of the computer lab, and looked in the door. He saw Carol, sitting at one of the computers, crying. It appeared that she was typing something.

David didn't know what to do. Part of him wanted to go inside, but another part of him said to leave her alone and just go home. He shook the feeling off and stepped into the room.

"Carol," David said. "I'm sorry." He leaned up against the wall and closed his eyes. "I actually thought that it would be a good idea, to get out how I felt. I guess I was wrong. I shouldn't have done it. I know that there's no sense in trying to talk about it, our relationship is over. I just didn't want to admit it."

He heard a click and then the printer started up. He opened his eyes and saw Carol stand up. She walked over to the printer and picked up the printed paper. She silently walked over and handed David the paper. She looked at him like she was going to say something, but instead, she nodded and walked out of the computer lab.

He looked at the paper. He saw that it was a letter addressed to him. He folded the paper up and walked out of the computer lab. He walked down the hallway, to the lobby. He walked out the door and to his house. When he walked through the door, Brenda looked at the clock and then back at him.

"The school day's not over yet," Brenda said. "Why are you home early?"

David looked at her, disappointment filling his eyes. "Because I made an ass out of myself."

He walked into his room and pulled out the letter from his pocket. He sat down on his bed and laid down. He opened the letter, and began to read.

"Dear David," the letter said. "I'd like to begin by saying that I am, at least a little, sorry about not speaking to you in so long. It's just hard, you know? I mean it went from 'I want to see him every day' to 'I don't ever want to see him again' in less than twenty four hours. I think you need to know, before I say much more, that you're right, we won't ever be together again. You really screwed up. But, besides being my first boyfriend (who happened to break my heart) you were also the only best friend I've ever had, and that hurts. That hurts because part of me wants nothing to do with you, but the other part of me really hopes that we can get through this eventually and be able to be friends again."

There was no, 'from Carol', it just ended. David reread it one more time to make sure that he hadn't missed anything. He put the letter on his desk and closed his eyes. It didn't matter to him that they weren't together anymore, or even that they weren't friends. The fact that she wanted to be friends again eventually was good enough.

David took a deep breath and fell into a peaceful sleep, dreaming about the friendship that he and Carol would have.

CHAPTER 11

William sat in a local coffee shop, grading papers and sipping a latte. He finished grading one, and rubbed his eyes. He looked out the window onto Main Street, and watched cars going by. Some of the cars were going by so quickly that William barely had time to see what color they were.

Those cars made him think of his life. Speeding by so quickly that he could barely see the colors. He took another sip of his latte and looked at the table. He saw that he still had three papers to grade before tomorrow. He set down the latte and rubbed his eyes. He leaned back in his chair and thought about his college days.

Even in his wildest fantasies, not to mention stories he had written, he had never actually pictured himself settled down, nonetheless with a wife and a child on the way. He smiled, thinking of all the times that he had gone out to the bar and proclaimed that he would "never have children" because of all the complications that come with them.

He still held this feeling to an extent, but he was actually really excited to have a child. He thought about the upcoming summer, where he would have time to finally sit down and look for a publisher for his book, something that he'd that he had taken an indefinite break from while the school year was still in session. Surprisingly, for the first time in a long time, Erica was the last thing to come to his thoughts.

In the two weeks that she had been pregnant, he had tried to be supportive of her in her time of need. The mood swings, however, had nearly drove him mad. He had started coming to this coffee shop every Thursday night, just to give each other much needed time alone.

William had made the mistake of telling his mother, who had told him that it sounded too much like they were going to break up. He had explained that it was good for both of them, and that all that was really going on was that they both needed one night a week to just have a separate work space away from one another. It didn't feel anything like they were headed for a break up to either of them. In fact, it had actually brought them closer together. Each Thursday night, when William returned, they hugged and kissed each other and headed to bed together, smiling and holding hands.

That in mind, William looked at his watch and saw that it was 9:30. He was tired, and much ready to get back home. He took a deep breath and did something he barely ever did. He put a solid 'B' on all three of the remaining papers and packed them all up into his backpack. He swallowed the rest of his latte and stood up.

He walked outside to his car and began driving back home.

When he got home, he walked inside, where Erica was sitting at the kitchen table, sipping tea.

"Hey, babe," William said.

"Hey," Erica said, smiling. "How was your evening?"

"It was good," William said, failing to relay how she hadn't made it to his immediate thoughts.

"Ready for bed?" Erica asked, stretching.

"Yes," William yawned.

Erica piled up her graded papers and put them in her bag. She stood up and took William's hand and they walked toward their bedroom.

They walked in, shut off the light and got into their bed. They kissed each other and they fell asleep.

The next morning, William and Erica rode to work together, refreshed.

"Hey, this is kind of old news now," William said. "But have you heard about David and Carol?"

"Yeah," Erica sighed. "I did."

"What do you think about it?" William said.

"I don't know," Erica said. "He *did* cheat on her. But they're teenagers. I like them both a lot, but let's face it, they're blowing the whole thing a bit out of proportion."

"I feel the same way," William said. "I mean, whether or not he cheated on her isn't the problem. He's a teenage boy. His hormones are raging. He's horny."

They both laughed out loud as William pulled into the driveway of the high school.

"You're awful," Erica said, still laughing.

"No," William said. "I'm *realistic.*"

They laughed once again and stepped out of the car. They walked inside and went to their classrooms, preparing for their days.

David walked into the school and started walking down the hall toward Mr. Morrison's room. He looked up and saw Carol, getting some things from her locker. He took in a deep breath and walked toward her.

"Hey," David said to Carol.

Carol hesitated. "Hello."

"Well this is uncomfortable," David nervously chuckled.

They both shared a short laugh.

"Look, Carol," David said. "I just want to talk. It seems like we should."

"Okay," Carol said. "What do you want to talk about?"

"I don't know," David sighed. "I miss you. Not like that, I mean, I'm not trying to be creepy. But I miss talking to you."

"Yeah," Carol said, sighing. "I know what you mean. It's like we saw each other all the time and now we don't."

"Do you think we could try to be friends," David said. "You know, not dating, just friends."

"I'd like that," Carol said, smiling.

"Okay, great," David said, smiling. "Do you want to go see a movie or something this weekend?"

"Doesn't that sound kind of like a date?" Carol asked.

"Kind of," David said. "But it's some action/science fiction movie. Not exactly date material."

They both laughed.

"Okay," Carol said. "It's *not* a date."

They both laughed again and walked to Mr. Morrison's classroom.

William noticed that David and Carol walked into the classroom together, laughing. He took a sip of his coffee and watched them. They sat down next to each other and appeared to be talking as though nothing had ever happened.

Interesting, William thought. *I wonder what's up with them?*

He thought about teenage life. Such an odd, complicated time of life. He chuckled at himself, then laughed out loud. He looked down at his desk when he saw students watching him.

Wow, William thought. *They just don't get it.*

The remainder of the week went well. David and Carol were like old friends, acting as though nothing had even happened between them. They talked during homeroom, hung out during break and took walks after school, talking about anything that they could think of.

Friday came and they decided to hang out at David's house until the movie, at six o'clock.

To say that David wasn't tempted a couple of times to kiss Carol would be a lie, but it would also be a lie to say that Carol hadn't felt the same feelings. They sat in the living room, watching TV.

They talked, but it was mostly about how their school weeks had been. They were both a bit tense, because it was the first time that they had been together at one of their houses since they had broken up. They both smiled though, enjoying the time together.

David looked at the clock and saw that it was five thirty. They got up and put on their shoes and coats. They began walking down town, to the movie theater. They didn't talk much on the way, because they were more concentrated on walking fast so that they could stay warm.

They got to the theater and walked inside.

"Two tickets," David said to the man. "And a medium popcorn?"

"Yeah, sounds good," Carol said.

"Alright," David said. "And two medium Pepsi's."

Carol felt a bit uncomfortable that David was paying for her, but she knew that the money had most likely come from Brenda anyway, so that helped. The man gave them their popcorn and drinks and they walked into the theater. They found a seat about three rows from the back.

They took off their coats and draped them over the backs of their seats, then they sat down.

They each took a sip of their Pepsi, then they started eating the popcorn.

David started looking around, to see if he knew anyone else there.

"Hey, look," David said. "There's Mr. Morrison and Miss Young."

Carol looked. Sure enough, William and Erica were walking in, hand in hand. They walked to the middle row and sat down.

"Hey, want to go see if we can sit with them?" Carol said.

"Yeah, sure," David said. "Let's go."

"Do you understand those two," William asked.

"What do you mean," Erica replied.

"I mean, he cheated on her, and now they're all friendly again," William said. "Are they stupid?"

Erica was making a gesture that indicated he should stop talking. Confused, he turned around to see David and Carol standing there.

"Hey," David and Carol said, simultaneously.

"Hey," William said, looking at them with a weird look on his face.

He still wasn't sure what was going on between them.

"Can we sit next to you," David asked.

"Yes, of course," Erica said, before William had time to respond.

He really didn't want them to sit there. Not because they were students, but because this was the first date night that Erica and he had had for a while. But Erica was too nice to say "no".

They sat down as they had before, draping their coats over their seats.

"So," William said, a bit uneasily. "How are you?"

They both said they were good and started eating their popcorn.

"Are you sure?" William said.

"William," Erica said.

"What," William said. "I'm just wondering."

"It's fine, really," David said.

"I'm just confused," William said. "I thought you two were broken up."

"We are," David said.

"Yeah," Carol said. "We're just friends."

"But I don't understand, he-"

"Hey, wasn't the movie supposed to start at six thirty?" Erica interrupted. "It's already six thirty five." She was giving William a look.

He stopped talking and turned his attention to the screen. The lights went down and the movie started.

Everything went well for about a half hour, David and Carol finished their popcorn and sodas and set the cups in the popcorn bucket on the floor.

Suddenly, the lead character was in a bedroom with a particularly sexy looking alien. Things started getting a bit steamy as they made their way to the bed.

William was squirming around in his seat. Usually this kind of scene would make him quite hot as well, and would be the perfect opportunity to steal a quick kiss from Erica. Usually, however, he didn't have students to his left, possibly watching. So he stared at the screen uncomfortably and breathed in heavily, trying to relax.

David was uncomfortable as well, but the difference was that he *was* getting hot. Beads of sweat had began appearing on his brow and things were also happening between his legs.

Without thinking, he finally turned his head, toward Carol, and leaned in, kissing her on the lips.

She kissed him back for a couple of seconds, but then, realizing what she was doing, what *he* was doing, she pushed him back.

"David," she said. "You can't do this. *We* can't do this. I thought you just wanted to be friends."

"I-I," David stammered. He put his head in his hands.

Carol stood up. "Maybe this was a bad idea," she said. "I'm going to go home."

She walked toward the exit and David stood up. "Wait, come back," he said.

He walked after her.

"Well," William whispered after they had gone. "That was a bit uncomfortable."

"It was only uncomfortable while they were here," Erica said, leaning in and kissing him.

"Carol," David said, when they got to the lobby. "I'm really sorry. It's just that scene-"

"I understand," Carol said. "But if that's the way we still feel about each other, maybe we shouldn't hang out. Bad things could happen."

David looked at her. He couldn't disagree. He nodded his head.

"I'm going home," Carol said, turning and walking out.

David turned around and walked back to the theater. He figured he might as well finish the movie. He got a seat in the back and watched the remainder of the film. He decided to get his coat after the film. He saw William and Erica kissing.

"At least someone's getting some action," David mumbled, moving his eyes up to the screen.

A long, torturous week went by after that, and both David and Carol were both starting to miss each other once again. Carol sat in her room, trying desperately to finish a paper that was due the next morning.

She stared at her laptop, but she didn't see any of the words which were looking back at her. She was too busy thinking about David. Her I-Pod headphones were in her ears and some ridiculously sappy love song was blaring in her ears. Tears were welling up in her eyes, but she fought them back.

This is so stupid she thought. *There's literally no reason for me to be crying. But goddamn it, why can't we just be friends?*

She thought that it would have been a lot better if they hadn't ever started dating, and she gritted her teeth and let out a "GRRR!" She saved her paper and set her laptop on the table next to her. She flopped down on her bed, a new sappy love song now blaring in her ears, and closed her eyes. She took a deep breath and softly fell asleep.

David felt like a total ass. *You're an idiot*, David had kept thinking to himself ever since he had left the movie theater. He sat at his desk, trying to do math homework, but instead he was staring out the window.

I just wanted to be friends with her again, David thought. *I miss the talks we had, the way we could tell her everything, her lips-*

David shook his head at that last thought.

Friends. FRIENDS, he yelled at himself mentally, hoping that thinking about it really loud would actually get it through his head and he would be able to just be friends with Carol. David took a deep breath.

"Love is a hard concept to understand," he said. He looked back down at his desk and continued his math homework.

The next day started about the same as they all had since David and Carol had gone out on their 'not a date'. David walked through the door as he always had and walked to his locker as he always had. He put his backpack in his locker as he always had, and walked into Mr. Morrison's class. He sat down and stared up ahead at the whiteboard.

Carol was already sitting there, up in the front, playing with her hair, trying to hide the fact that she had seen David walk in. David looked over and noticed that she was fidgeting with her hair, not to mention her legs were moving around as though she were nervous for some unknown reason.

Finally, David saw her look down and take a deep breath. She stood up and turned around. She walked back by David and sat next to him. She didn't say anything, but she looked over at him and smiled and quickly turned away.

David couldn't help but also notice that Mr. Morrison had taken a slight interest, and was staring back, moving his eyes back and forth to the two of them. After a few seconds, he closed his eyes and shook his head. He looked back at his desk and started writing things.

"David," Carol finally said. "How are you doing?"

"I'm doing well," David said quietly. "And you?"

"I'm doing decent," Carol said. "Um, I think we should talk."

"Yeah," David said. "Maybe we should."

"What do you think we should do?" Carol asked. "It sounds corny, but it's like I can't stop thinking about you."

Mr. Morrison let out something that sounded like a snicker, but David wasn't sure if he had heard right.

"I know what you mean," David said. "But is it even *possible* for us to be friends?"

"I'd like to think it is," Carol said. "But I guess only time will tell."

Mr. Morrison stood up, holding back laughter and said "Class, I'll be right back."

He walked across the hall to Erica's room and walked in. Her homeroom students looked up, not all that surprised to see him, and went back to doing whatever they had been doing before he had gotten there.

"Erica," William said. "Can I chat with you out in the hall?"

"Of course," Erica said. "Is something wrong?"

"Not to the extent that you should be worried," William said.

"Okay," Erica said, confused. She got up and followed him out into the hallway.

"Our little 'love birds' David and Carol are back at it again," William said.

"William," Erica said. "They're not *our* love birds and they're not *our* problem."

"I know," William said, staring at the floor thoughtfully. He looked back up at her. "And I know that it sounds ridiculous, but they're going to hurt each other and they don't even realize it."

"So what do you suggest, we sit down and have a chat," Erica asked. "We're not psychiatrists."

"Again, I know," William said. "But I think we could really do some good here. I could tell them to meet us back here for lunch. We could talk then."

"Alright," Erica said. "If you really think that it will help, I'm there for you."

"Thanks babe," William said, kissing her on the cheek.

"No problem," Erica said.

William turned around and walked back into his room just as the bell rang.

The students started piling out and William said, "David, Carol, can you come here for a moment?"

The two of them nervously walked up to his desk.

"Could the two of you meet Erica and I in here at lunch time?" William asked.

Without saying a word, they both nodded. Then they left.

"See you then," William said. "And don't bring anything from the cafeteria, lunch is on me."

Around ten thirty, William called the local pizza place and ordered a large pizza. He had a free period, so he was able to drive down and get it. While he was in town, he stopped at the grocery store and grabbed a large bottle of soda and some plastic cups. Then he went back to the school and went to his classroom.

He cleared off his desk and set down the pizza. Just as he was pouring the drinks, David and Carol walked in, Erica right behind them.

"Impressive," Erica said, sarcastically. "I wish you treated me *this* good."

William tried to give her a 'shut up' look, but couldn't help but smile.

"You can all grab a cup and some pizza and then if you would, take a seat," William said, realizing how ridiculous he sounded.

"Alright," William said, after David and Carol sat down. "I don't like to interfere with my students' lives, but as long as we all have to see each other every day, I think it's fair that we're all on terms that don't make us wonder what the hell is going on. That being said, I'd like you to tell me, one at a time, what is going on between you two. David, you may go first, seeing as you're the cause of all of this."

"Well," David said, blushing. "I don't have to tell you what I did, you already know that, but I will say that it ended in us breaking up. So, we decided to try to be friends, which, as you know because of the movie theater incident, didn't go so well. But, the last week, at least for me, has been a living hell and I really want to try to be friends with Carol again."

"Carol," William said. "Do you have anything to add?"

Carol shook her head 'no'.

"Okay, look," William said. "I think my biggest question is, why do you want to be friends?"

"Because," Carol said. "We were so happy together."

"You aren't convincing me," William said. "And your face is less than happy about it. I don't mean to sound blunt, but could it just be that you're both really horny?"

David and Carol's mouths both dropped and they looked away, embarrassed.

William took a breath. "Sorry," William said. "That came out sounding rude and invasive, not at all what I was going for."

"I think what William's trying to say," Said Erica, jumping in to save William. "Is that we've both been teenagers, and we understand what it's like. Your first boyfriend or girlfriend, not to mention the person you lost your virginity to, will always be important to you, no matter how old you get or how many relationships you have. That won't ever change. They'll always be in the back of your mind. You'll wonder where they are, what they're up to, if they ever found love, if they have kids, whatever, you get my point. And I know it's hard, but when it's over, it's over, you've got to understand that. Some relationships don't last, that's life. And sometimes, trying to mend them back together only makes things worse. So, is it possible to still be friends? Yes, but you've got to give it more time than you have. It's hard, but you have to get over each other as far as your relationship goes first. Do you understand?"

"Yes," David and Carol both said, nodding.

"Okay, good," Erica said, smiling. "I think we're done here, but you're both more than welcome to stay and finish the pizza and soda."

Erica walked over and got herself a cup of soda and a slice of pizza and began eating.

David and Carol both had smiles on their faces, as they ate their pizza.

William and Erica sat next to each other, heads against each others', watching the two teenagers, who were no doubt thinking of the friendship that had once been and the friendship that it may once again be.

"Erica," Carol said finally.

"Yes, Carol," Erica said.

"How long will it take?"

"Time will tell, Carol," Erica replied. "Time will tell."

CHAPTER 12

It was March now, only three months away from the end of David and Carol's Freshman year. They had certainly had quite an eventful one. They spent two days talking over what Erica had told them and finally, they figured out what they needed to do.

It was a hard decision, but nevertheless one that needed to be made. David and Carol had actually asked Erica to write up a fake contract, stating that they were to take a month off of speaking, for them to sign. Erica and William had both signed as witnesses. Erica had even gone to principal Jodi's office and arranged for Carol to be moved to her homeroom and English class.

Things were moving along smoothly. David and Carol hadn't talked, as the contract had said. Neither of them would have believed it if they had been told prior to signing the contract, but they were both feeling better and more relaxed about life since they had signed it. They were still on each others minds, but Erica said that was to be expected. The important thing to remember, she had said, was that despite the thoughts in their heads, it was time to move on.

They both took their newly found alone time to work on their writing, which they had both improved on through the mentoring of William and Erica. David found that taking long strolls through town on his own made for great ways to get new ideas processed, as well as personal thoughts.

Carol had began cooking, which is something that she hadn't really considered in the past, but like David's walks, she found that cooking was a great tool for relaxing and thinking about life.

They had also both started opening up to more people around them, considering that they didn't have each other to talk about anymore. David had befriended Tim, a guy in his English class and a fellow writer.

"That's love," Tim said, when David had finally explained everything about Carol. "I mean, it's not your fault that you cheated. I've seen the girl you cheated with, irresistible. Any guy would have done the same thing in your position."

David couldn't help but laugh. Tim was a pretty funny guy, even if he was a bit cynical.

That weekend, Tim and David had gone to the movies, even though they had no idea what the movie was about. They sat in the back row, and noticed immediately that Carol was sitting down in front, all alone.

"So you're really not allowed to even speak to her for a whole month," Tim inquired.

"No," David said. "And it actually feels great."

"That's awesome, man," Tim said. The subject was dropped, and instead Tim began telling David about a sci-fi comedy story about a female alien who comes to earth and falls in love with the first guy she sees.

William was having severe second thoughts as to why he had asked Erica to marry him. He did love her, and he was glad that they were together, but no one had told him that getting married was so much work.

"I don't care what color the theme is," he said, half yelling at Erica.

"Well you have to help me figure it out so we can start buying decorations," Erica said.

"Wait a minute," William said. "What do you mean *we*?"

"It's not just *my* wedding," Erica said, chuckling. "I thought that we could plan it and shop for it together."

"Yeah," William said, forcing a smile. "That's a great idea. I can't wait, really. Do you want some coffee?"

"Sure, I'd love some, honey," Erica said.

"Good," William said. "I'll make some."

He brewed the coffee and poured Erica a glass. He handed it to her, and when she wasn't looking, he pulled out a bottle of vodka and poured enough in the cup for half a glass. Then he filled the rest with coffee and sat down at the table.

"Look at this color," Erica said, pointing to a page in the catalog she was reading.

"It's nice," William said, smiling.

"Just nice?" Erica asked. "I think it's beautiful."

"Beautiful," William said, smiling. "I think that's a bit of a stretch. *That's* beautiful."

"That's black," Erica said. "Why would you want a black themed wedding?"

"I, uh, well, I don't know," William stammered. He looked at his watch. "We've got to get going to work. That way we can go shopping later."

Erica wasn't impressed. It *was* time for work, but she knew that he was only using it as an excuse.

"If you don't want to help me with this, why don't you just tell me," she asked. "I'll understand."

"It's complicated," William said. "I want to spend time with you, and at the same time, this isn't really my thing. I'm sorry. Look, I want to help. I mean it. Let's go Friday after work."

"Okay," Erica said, smiling, standing up and noticing the clock. "Let's get to work."

Carol had an awful cold and Alice had told her that she wasn't going to school today.

"I'm fine mom, really," Carol had said.

"I understand," Alice said. "But you don't look it and you don't sound it. Stay home and rest today. It should be gone by tomorrow."

Carol went into her room and sprawled out on her bed. She stared at the blank white ceiling. She was immediately bored. School wasn't the greatest place on earth, but at least it kept her busy.

She picked up a notebook from her bedside table and opened it up. She had been writing out an outline to what would hopefully become her first book, a mystery-romance novel. She was still trying to come up with a few options as to what the killer's motive was. She had read about three Agatha Christie books to help prepare and she had a short list of others that she still wanted to read before she actually started writing the book.

She had writers block, which she thought was funny since she wasn't even actually writing anything. She turned on her TV and tuned into some old sitcom. Then she put the notebook back on the table and fell asleep.

David hadn't even noticed that Carol wasn't at school. He was too busy throwing around a new plot in his own head. It wasn't anywhere near a book, but he had found a local writing contest in the newspaper and had decided to write something and submit it.

Throughout the day, he jotted down notes on his various notebooks for different classes. When he got home, he would rewrite all of the notes in a separate notebook and hopefully get started on the story.

During his last class of the day, Biology, he actually had yelled out "yes" because he had come up with a fantastic way to end the story. Embarrassed, he slunk down in his chair and quickly jotted down the scene in his Biology notebook.

The final bell rang and he put his notebook into his backpack and stood up. He walked into the hallway, toward his locker, where he opened it up and, for the first time that year, he put all of his notebooks into his backpack. He walked toward the front lobby and started walking home to begin putting his story together.

By the end of the school day, Carol had finished her outline and was slowly writing out a prologue. It felt rough, but she was still proud of herself for finally starting her first book. She looked down at her outline and thought for a minute. She jotted down a note and then continued typing the prologue.

David wrote the first three pages within ten minutes and he hit the 'save' button. He sat back and looked at his computer, pride filling his heart. He decided to have a congratulatory soda and he walked out to the kitchen. He reached into the refrigerator and pulled out a cold one.

He walked back into his room and opened up the soda. He took a long swallow and set down the soda on his desk. He thought for a moment. He wrote one more line, hit 'save' again and closed out of the document. Not bad for the first day, he thought and he decided to take a nap. He guzzled down the rest of his soda and walked over to his bed and got in.

He was extremely proud of himself. He closed his eyes and thought about how much more pride he would feel once it was done. How proud Brenda would be. How much William and Erica would be. How proud Carol would be.

His eyes jolted open. He took a deep breath, trying to figure out why that thought had entered his head. He continued thinking about her, what she was doing at that time, what she may be writing. Tears formed in his eyes and began slowly trickling down his face.

He tried fighting them back, but finally just let them fall. He missed her, there was no doubt about that. He gave himself a mental pat on the back because he had lasted so long without even thinking about her. He wiped the tears from his eyes and closed them, quickly falling asleep.

On Friday, after the final bell of the day, William and Erica walked out into the parking lot and got into William's car. They were headed to a local wedding shop, that, according to advertisement, had everything that would be needed for their wedding.

It was a thirty minute drive to the shop, and they went over some last minute ideas, the kind of cake, the colors, what color William's tuxedo should be. William had expected to see Erica's mother waiting for them, but when they got there, he got a surprise.

"Mom," William said. "What are you doing here?"

"I love you too, William," Kathleen said.

"I love you, Mom," William said. "But what are you doing here?"

"Helping," Kathleen said. "Mona called me this morning and said that you two were coming to start wedding shopping."

"I was quite surprised to hear that you hadn't called her," Mona said.

"It must have slipped our minds," William said.

"Let's go inside," Erica said.

They walked inside the party shop, where they saw decorations from wall to wall. They were all in awe, and were marveling at the amount of different decorations. A clerk saw them and began walking over.

"Soon to be newlyweds, I presume," she said with a smile. "I could tell by the way you were looking at everything. You must be their mothers?"

"Yes," Mona said.

"Well," the clerk said. "My name is Nancy, and I'd be happy to help you in any way possible. What is your theme?"

"We actually aren't really sure," Erica said. "We were hoping to get some ideas. We want a nice wedding, but we also want it affordable."

"Okay," Nancy said. "Well, not to gloat, but I always start by telling people about my wedding. We had it on a beach, nothing special really, but then we went back to my in laws' cabin on the lake and had the reception. It was affordable, fun and memorable."

"How lovely," Kathleen said, with a thoughtful grin. "Our wedding was at a church, and the reception was held in the parking lot." She nodded and looked at William. "Cheap guy, your father."

"Another popular wedding," Nancy said, not missing a beat, "is a wedding in a large, green field. But here, we specialize in personalized weddings. We'll take your hobbies, likes, and help create a wedding that suits you. We had a couple last year who both traveled a lot, so we thought it might be a fun idea to have a wedding on a plane."

"That's neat," Erica said, amazed.

"Not so much," Nancy said. "There was a bit of turbulence, and a *lot* of alcohol. It wasn't pretty."

"I think we'll just go with a regular outside summer wedding," Erica said, trying to smile.

"Okay," Nancy said. "Let me go run some numbers on basic items and I'll get back to you in a few minutes. Feel free to peruse."

"Thank you," Erica said.

Nancy walked back to the cash register, where she had a notebook, and started jotting things down and typing into a calculator.

"I'm so happy, William," Erica said.

"Me too," William admitted, smiling. "I hadn't really put much thought into it, honestly, but being here, looking at this stuff, it makes it that more real."

They walked around, looking at different items they might want for the wedding. Erica picked up a few small things, but nothing large. She had decided that she didn't really want a big wedding.

They heard a printer and turned around. Nancy stapled three pieces of paper and walked over to them.

"Okay," Nancy said, folding up the papers. "I'm going to be honest with you. I usually tell people to take these home and go over them there. These papers contain an *approximate* price, but it can still freak some people out. We don't like people getting violent in the stores, it causes items to break and such, and then their cost *really* goes up. I included the price of a basic wedding cake, with a picture as well."

"Thank you again," Erica said. "We'll be back. Do you do catering as well?"

"We don't personally," Nancy said. "But we have connections."

They all said goodbye and walked outside. William and Erica said goodbye to their mothers and got into their car. They decided to put the papers away and look at them once they were home.

"Let's go out for dinner," William said.

"Really," Erica said, smiling.

"Yeah," William replied, also smiling.

They drove to the nearest city and went to a fairly fancy restaurant. William parked the car and they went inside.

"Seating for two," the host asked.

"Yes," William said, smiling.

They were seated and started looking at the menu.

"So," Erica said. "How much do you think it will cost?"

"That depends on what you order," William said. "I mean the prices are pretty decent here."

"Not here," Erica said. "I meant the wedding."

William smiled. "I know what you meant. Don't worry about it."

"I just don't want it to be too much," Erica said.

"Erica," William said. "Even if it cost me a million dollars, it wouldn't be enough. There isn't enough money on this planet that could equal what you're worth to me."

Erica started crying. "That's the nicest thing that anyone has ever said to me."

"It's true," William said, smiling back across the table.

"I have my ultrasound on Monday," Erica reminded him.

"I can't wait," William said. "The first glimpse at our baby."

William seemed to drift away a bit.

"What is it," Erica asked.

"Everything," William said. "Within a year, I'm going to be a family man. I just never thought that would happen. It makes me very happy."

Erica reached over and touched his hand. "It makes me very happy too."

She smiled at him and they looked back at their menu's, trying to figure out what to order.

Saturday, David woke up and turned over, looking at his clock. It said it was ten thirty and David sat up. He walked out of his room and said "good morning" to Brenda. Then he picked up the phone and dialed Tim's number.

"Hello," Tim's mom answered.

"Hey," David said. "Is Tim there?"

"I think he's still sleeping, just a second," his mom said. David heard footsteps, no doubt headed for Tim's bedroom. This was followed by "Tim, wake up you have a phone call."

David heard Tim's voice, mumbling audible sounds, then "Hello?"

"Hey," David said. "It's David. Sorry to wake you up, just wanted to know if we were still going to the movies tonight."

"Is there anything else to do in this town?" Tim asked.

"If only," David said. "If you want, I can ask Brenda if you can come back here after. We could order a pizza and hang out over here tonight."

"Sounds like a plan, man," Tim said. "I'll see you later."

"Later," David said, hanging up the phone.

David went to the kitchen and made himself a ham and cheese sandwich with onions and pickles. Then he grabbed a Pepsi from the refrigerator and walked back to his room. He set his sandwich and Pepsi on a table next to his desk and opened up his story and began writing.

That night, it seemed, like it always did, that everyone in town was going to the movies. Like Tim had said on the phone, there wasn't much to do in town, so everyone flocked to the movie theater on weekends, even if it was a 'B' level romantic comedy like this one.

David and Tim were standing in line and Tim was telling him about the story he was working on.

"Weren't you telling me about this the last time we were here?" David asked.

"Yes," Tim said, laughing. "But I hadn't started writing it yet. Now I've got five pages done. You're in it, by the way."

"Really," David said.

"Yeah," Tim said. "The lead character is modeled after me, and every lead character needs a best friend, right?"

"Yeah," David said. "Thanks for including me. I'll try to throw you into the one I'm writing now if I find a spot."

They had made their way to the front of the line and they bought their tickets, a small popcorn each and a medium soda. They walked into the theater and sat at their usual spot, in the back.

"Look who it is," Tim said, pointing to the front.

"Carol's here again," David said. "It's like a curse, I can't get away from her."

"You know, I can't really tell, but it looks like she's here with somebody," Tim said, squinting his eyes.

"That's cool," David said after a short hesitation. "I mean, she can do whatever she wants."

"Are you going to be alright," Tim asked. "Because we can leave if you want and watch a movie at your place."

"No," David said. "We've already paid. I'll be fine."

Five minutes later, the theater got dark and the movie started.

David tried his hardest to enjoy the movie, but he couldn't help but keep looking at Carol and her date. David didn't know how long they had known each other, but figured it couldn't have been long. Yet, he was staring at the two of them, holding hands, giggling and generally having a good time.

David finally closed his eyes, took a deep breath and opened his eyes back up. He was able to calm himself down enough so that he could enjoy the rest of the movie.

After the movie ended, David and Tim got up and walked out to the lobby.

"I've got to go to the bathroom, I'll be right back," Tim said.

David watched Tim walk into the bathroom and leaned against a wall to wait for him. David yawned, but shook it off. He leaned his head back and closed his eyes. He remembered that Tim and him were going to order a pizza when they got back to his house, which made him happy. He hadn't eaten supper yet and his stomach was hurting.

"Ready to go," Tim asked.

David opened his eyes and saw Tim. He was about to say "yes", when he saw Carol and her date walk out of the theater. Tim turned, following his gaze.

"Come on," Tim said, gently touching David's shoulder and pushing him softly toward the door.

"Hello, David," Carol said.

Tim closed his eyes, annoyed and afraid and looked at David, who actually looked pretty calm.

"Hey," David said.

"How have you been," Carol asked.

What's she up to, Tim thought, paying close attention to her behavior.

"I've been good," David said. "The movie was pretty good."

"I thought it sucked," said Carol's date. "I hate that sappy shit."

"This is Sean," Carol said quickly. "My date. I didn't care for it that much either."

David shot her an odd look. She had never struck him as the type to absolutely *love* romantic comedies, but she had seemed to have enjoyed it enough when they had gone on their first date.

"David, we've got to go," Tim said. "If we're going to make it back to your place and order that pizza we should go."

"Yeah," David said, as though he had forgotten completely about the pizza. "Goodbye, Carol."

"Goodbye," she said, as David and Tim walked outside.

"Well that was uncomfortable," Tim said. "I mean that guy's just-"

"I don't want to talk about it," David said. "I'm fine, really. I just don't want to talk about it."

"Okay," Tim said. "Well we can if you want, just know that."

They didn't say much else for the rest of the walk. Usually, after watching a movie, they would take the time to talk about it, but there wasn't much to talk about. It was pretty generic. Boy meets girl, they have some funny interactions, a few awkward dates, they live happily ever after. Not too much originality to it.

As soon as they were in the kitchen, David picked up the phone and dialed the number for the pizza place.

"Hello," David said. "I'd like to have two medium supreme pizzas. The name's David Craven. Okay, thank you."

David hung up the phone and told Tim that it would be fifteen minutes. They walked into the living room and turned on the TV.

Carol hadn't met Sean at school, but instead when she had been walking around the mall with Alice. They had both been in a store together, and ended up talking about writing. It wasn't exactly a relationship, but they had gone out a couple of times.

Carol wasn't sure if she wanted a relationship with Sean. It was nice to have a friend to talk to, especially one with similar interests, but he was kind of a jerk.

That night after the movies, they walked out to Sean's car.

"So who was that," Sean asked.

"He was my boyfriend for a while," Carol admitted. "We tried to be friends after we broke up, but it didn't work out."

"Why did you break up," Sean asked.

"He cheated on me at a party," Carol said.

"I would never cheat on you, Carol," Sean said.

He leaned in and kissed Carol, and she allowed it for a few seconds. Then, she pushed him away.

"What," Sean said.

"I don't want to do this," Carol said. "We've only known each other for a couple of weeks."

"Sorry," Sean said. "My problem is that I'm always too forward."

"It's okay," Carol said. "I'm just not ready for anything like that. I don't mean to sound rude, but I think I'm going to walk home if that's okay with you."

"Yeah, sure," Sean said. "I'll call you in a few days."

Carol nodded and got out of the car.

"Goodbye," she said.

"Bye," Sean said.

Carol closed the door and turned around. She began walking toward her house.

The night before St. Patrick's Day, Robert had called William and asked if him and Erica would want to come to a party at his house. William had asked Erica and once she said yes, and William had called him back and told him. William and Erica agreed that it would be fun, as well as a bit funny, considering that they had met at one of Robert's parties. Lilly would also be there, which was fine by Erica, because she hadn't seen Lilly in some time. The party was going to begin at eight o'clock.

William and Erica got into the car and started driving toward Robert's house.

"So," William said. "Lilly's going to be there?"

"Yeah," Erica said happily. "Her and Robert have been going out since we had our double date with them."

"That's good," William said. "Robert needs some stability in his life."

They pulled into Robert's driveway and saw that there were quite a few guests there already. They got out of the car and walked up to the door. William knocked.

"Hey," Robert said as he approached the door. "Come on in. There's a keg in the living room and a full cooler in the kitchen."

"Thanks for the information," William said. "How have you been?"

"Oh, you know, the usual," Robert said. "Working, sleeping, dating." Robert smiled. "I really want to thank you two for taking us with you that night."

"You're welcome," Erica said. "Where *is* Lilly, anyway?"

"She's in the living room, socializing," Robert said.

"Okay, thank you," Erica said. She walked toward the living room. William and Robert heard her and Lilly say how much they had missed each other.

"Let's go get you a beer," Robert said.

They walked into the kitchen and Robert reached into a cooler and pulled out a beer.

"Here you go," Robert said, handing it to William.

"Thank *you*," William said, opening the beer and taking a sip.

"You're welcome," Robert said, chuckling. "So, only a couple of months left until you'll be walking down the aisle."

"Yeah, I know," William said. "I can hardly believe it, time does fly."

"It's so funny," Robert said, taking a sip of beer.

"What is," William asked.

"I remember in college," Robert said. "You said you refused to get married and have any children. Now you're about to do both."

William looked down at the floor nervously and took another sip of beer. "Yeah, I guess I am."

"Hey," Robert said. "Don't get nervous on me now. It's a great thing. I'm really happy for you."

"Thanks man," William said. "I guess I just hadn't really taken the time to think about it all as a whole yet."

"You're going to be a great husband," Robert said. "And an even better father. I guarantee that. Now, let's go find our ladies."

"Alright," William said, smiling. "Let me just grab a soda for Erica."

He grabbed a soda out of the refrigerator and they headed toward the living room, where Erica and Lilly were sitting on the couch, chuckling at an already drunk couple try to dance.

"Hey, ladies," Robert said.

"Hey," Lilly and Erica said.

"Honey," Erica said. "If I ever get *that* drunk, don't let me dance."

"Noted," William said, laughing.

"Since you're not drunk now, would you like to dance," William asked.

"Of course," Erica said, standing up.

William set his beer and Erica's soda on the table next to the couch and stood back up. He wasn't much of a dancer, but he did his best, which wasn't saying much.

"When was the last time you danced, 1995," Robert said, laughing.

"Something like that," William said, laughing.

Robert sat down next to Lilly.

"I was going to ask you to dance, but watching these two is more fun," Robert said.

Lilly laughed. "Fun or not, you're dancing."

She stood up and pulled Robert up onto his feet and they both began dancing. They danced for half an hour, as Roberts' mix CD played rock music, dance music, slow music and other songs of variety.

They sat down after dancing for a while and relaxed. Robert switched CD's to an exclusively slow dance mix and they watched all of the other couples try to dance with one another.

"This reminds me of college," Robert said, looking at William. "Remember that party we ended up at our Freshman year?"

"You mean the party that we shouldn't have been anywhere near?" William said back, taking a sip.

"Yeah," Robert said. "That one."

"So, these guys come up to us in the dining hall," William said, looking at Erica and Lilly. "And they ask us if we want to go to a party. We're Freshmen in college, so of course, we said 'yes'. They hand us this piece of paper with a time and address on it. So about two hours later, we start walking across town to where this party is. We walk in, and all of the guests are looking at us like they know, before we even know, that we shouldn't be there. Robert, being Robert, immediately spots a keg and we make our way to it and help ourselves to some beer. We walked toward some music we heard and there were people dancing everywhere. Do you want to take it from here? I know it's your favorite part."

"Yeah," Robert said., smiling slyly. "So we walk into this room, drinking like we own the place, and William here, starts asking girls, of all levels of intoxication, if they'd like to dance. I recall that one of them was even passed out. Finally, this girl comes up and asks us how old we are. Smart one Morrison actually *tells* this girl that we're only eighteen. So she takes our beers from us, with a concerned look on her face, and walks away. I think we're going to get in trouble, so I sit down on the couch which is only a couple of feet from where we were. William sits down next to me, and we're freaking out. We don't know where she went, we're thinking she's going to call the cops. So finally, she returns and hands each of us a soda. She says, 'have fun, boys' and walks away. We sat there, sipping our soda and watching drunk people, who no doubt got laid that night, dance in front of us. Finally, I got sick of it and told William we were leaving. That was the last time that I let him say *anything* when we went to a party."

Erica and Lilly were laughing uncontrollably by the end of the story.

"*Why* would you tell her that you were only eighteen," Erica asked.

"Because I was *eighteen*," William said, taking a sip of his beer.

Pretty soon, people started to fan out and there weren't many people left.

"I've noticed something," William said. "A lot of people come to your parties, but by the end there aren't many left."

"People come to meet people," Robert said. "Once they do that, they say 'screw the party' and take off. I have no problem with it at all. I provide a service."

"Well," William said. "I recall a time when you tried to provide a different kind of service. Also in college, if I remember correctly."

"Hey, come on, man," Robert said. "That was a one time thing."

"Yeah," William said. "So what? You had your fun, now let me have mine. I won't use that many words. There isn't much to say. In college, Robert thought he could make some easy money by creating a prostitute ring."

"What," Lilly burst out, laughing.

"He would stand on the street, asking girls if they'd like to make some money by servicing men," William said. "You should have seen what happened when the school newspaper found out. He almost got kicked out, but luckily, I stood up for him, saying he was an idiot, and the Dean let him stay."

"I think it's time for you to leave," Robert said, half serious.

"Oh, come on, man," William said. "That's one of my favorite college stories. My students love it!"

"You tell your students?" Robert said.

"No," William said, laughing. "But I got you to believe me."

"Actually," Erica said, laughing so hard she had tears coming out of her eyes. "We really should be going."

They all stood up and said goodbye to one another.

"Come over again sometime," Robert said. "Just for dinner or something."

"Will do," William said, stumbling outside to his car.

He got into the passenger's side and Erica got into the drivers' side and drove them home.

Monday, after work, they were driving to Erica's doctor's office for her first ultrasound.

"This is so exciting," Erica said. "We're going to see our baby for the first time."

"I know," William said, more excited than he was letting on.

"I read that we won't be able to tell whether or not it's a boy or girl yet," Erica said.

"Are you sure you want to know?" William asked. "What if we let ourselves be surprised."

"We have to know what we're buying for," Erica said.

"That's such an ancient way of thinking," William said, chuckling. "I don't know about you, but I don't want my kid growing up with stereotypes. I think we should wait and just buy what we think is adorable for a baby. And we can continue that as he, or she, grows up. We can let our child decide who it is. Whether that means being a gay male, a lesbian female, or a transgendered person. It doesn't matter."

"William," Erica said, tearing up. "I know that it may be implied, but I love you!"

She reached over and clutched William's hand and leaned over on his shoulder.

"And I agree," she said. "Who are we to say who our child is? I agree. Surprise it is."

William pulled into the driveway of Erica's doctor's office and they got out of the car.

They walked inside and Erica checked in. She was given a clipboard with a paper to fill out. She filled out the paper and handed it back to the receptionist. She sat back down with William and held his hand while they waited for the nurse to come out and get them.

The nurse came out and asked them to come in with her. She led them down a short hallway and into a small room.

"I'm just going to check your vitals," the nurse said.

She took Erica's blood pressure, checked her heart beat and listened to her belly.

"Everything's good," she said. "The doctor will be right in."

She left the room and within a minute, the doctor came in.

"Hello, hello," the doctor, Dr. Brooks said. "How are you today?"

"I'm good," Erica said. "We're really excited!"

"Well, hop up onto the table and we'll get started," Dr. Brooks said.

Erica and William stood up and William helped Erica get up onto the table. He helped her lay down slowly. The doctor then began the ultrasound. William and Erica saw the baby on the screen and both smiled at one another.

"Oh," Erica said. "It's probably too early to tell, but I want you to know that we don't want to know the sex of the baby when the time comes."

"Okay," Dr. Brooks said, smiling. "Surprise births are the best. You know, just for fun, my wife and I placed a bet to see who could guess the sex. We didn't care either way, but it was a fun way of getting through the pregnancy."

The doctor pushed a button, taking a snap shot for the two of them to take home. He did this three more times as he observed the fetus.

After about ten minutes, he was finished. He printed out the photos for Erica and William and handed them to Erica.

"Well," Dr. Brooks said. "I'd say your baby is quite healthy. The heart beat was a bit irregular, but it's nothing that I am concerned with right now. The receptionist will make you an appointment for your next ultrasound. Have a good day."

"An irregular heartbeat," Erica said once the doctor had gone out of the room.

"He said it's nothing to worry about," William said. "So don't worry. Remember, he's the professional."

"Still," Erica said. "I'm not sure I like how he said that."

"It will be fine," William said. "Let's go set up your next appointment."

"Okay," Erica said.

They walked out to the receptionist desk and set up Erica's next appointment. They walked out to the car and sat there for about ten minutes, just looking at the pictures of their child.

"It's amazing," Erica said.

"It's beautiful," William said.

"It's ours," Erica said, leaning over and kissing him on the cheek.

"Yes it is," William said. "By the way, I bet you ten bucks right now that it's a girl."

"You're on," Erica said, laughing.

William turned on the car and pulled out of the driveway. They drove back, in silence, amazed at what they had just seen. They couldn't wait to show all of their friends and family the first pictures of their child. The first picture of what would become their family.

CHAPTER 13

On the morning of April first, before the school day began, David and Carol met William and Erica in William's classroom. Their month was over, as their contract said, and they could try again, if they wanted, to be friends.

David was surprised, but the urge to be friends with Carol wasn't nearly as strong as he had thought that it would be. He was hanging out with Tim almost every weekend and he had seemingly filled the gap in David's life.

Carol didn't really care either way. She had found that having more to herself, while making her a social recluse, was very useful. She had more time for her writing, and was able to get her homework done way ahead of schedule, which was nice.

"Alright," Erica said, holding up the contract and looking at the two of them. "Your month away from each other is up. You may, if you wish, try to be friends once again."

She tore the contract up into about ten pieces and dropped the pieces into the recycling bin next to William's desk.

Neither David or Carol smiled at this, but instead just stood there. They turned and got into seats next to each other but did not talk at all. They began jotting down notes, for some story William guessed.

William motioned for Erica to follow him and they walked out into the hallway.

"Why aren't they talking," he asked Erica.

"It's just as I suspected," Erica said, smiling. "A month alone and they have either realized that they don't need each other or found other things to do instead of, well, each other."

"You mean you knew this would happen," William asked, looking back into his room, where they still were not speaking. "How did I find such an intelligent girl such as you?"

He kissed her on the cheek and they said their morning goodbyes and walked into their separate classrooms to prepare for their days.

William was sitting at his desk eating his lunch when he received a phone call from Robert. Normally, William wouldn't have answered his phone during work, but normally, Robert wouldn't call him at work unless it was something urgent.

"Hello," William said, a slight sound of nervousness in his voice.

"Hey," Robert said, enthusiastically. "Before you say anything, don't. I know it's about a month early, but oh well, we're going out next weekend to have your bachelor party."

"Bachelor party," William said. "I don't need one of those."

"That's what every generic man has said since the invention of bachelor parties," Robert said. "So shut up, it's not negotiable."

"Okay, fine," William said, rubbing his eyes. "Where are we going?"

"It's a surprise," Robert said slyly. "And I've been watching you closer than you think. I think you'll be pretty impressed with the guest list."

"Oh god," William said. "Who did you invite?"

"You'll see," Robert said. "I'll call you later."

He hung up the phone. William put his phone in his pocket and picked up his sandwich. He took a bite and then he looked to his right, through the doorway into Erica's room on the other side of the hallway.

Robert had said that all 'generic' guys said no to bachelor parties, no doubt because of what their fiance would say. He decided that he would tell Erica later, on the ride home.

David called Carol as soon as he got home from school.

"Hello," Alice answered.

"Hey," David said. "This is David, can I talk to Carol.?"

"Yeah," Alice said with a sigh. "Just a second."

A minute later, the phone was picked up again.

"David?" Carol said.

"Yeah," David said. "Look, we need to talk."

"I agree," Carol said.

"It's just that, even though our month long contract is up," David said. "And don't take this the wrong way-"

"You don't have the urge to hang out with me anymore," Carol said.

"Yeah," David said. "But how did you know-"

"I feel the same way," Carol said.

"Oh," David said. "Okay. I guess that's that then."

"Now hold on," Carol said. "I still consider you a friend, a great one. I just don't feel the urge to hang out with you romantically anymore."

"That's what I meant too," David said.

"So maybe later this week, we can get together for a walk or something," Carol said.

"Yeah," David said. "I'd like that. I'll talk to you later."

"Okay," Carol said. "Bye."

David hung up the phone and walked into his room, not sure how he felt about the situation.

"I think it's a great idea," Erica said, after William told her about the bachelor party.

"Really," William said.

"Honestly," Erica said. "Robert's right. Every man should have a bachelor party. I'd like to think that the fun doesn't stop at marriage, but *that* kind of fun definitely does. So yes, go out and have one more free night out with your friends."

"Okay," William said, smiling. "If you insist."

At school, David and Carol had once again discussed going for a walk after school one day that week. They had agreed on Thursday.

After school on Thursday, they met in the lobby of the high school and began their walk.

"So," Carol said as they walked down the driveway of the high school. "What have you been up to?"

"Writing mostly," David said. "And hanging out with Tim."

"I figured," Carol said. "I see you guys together all the time."

"He's an awesome guy," David said. "He's a writer too, we have a lot to talk about. And we both love movies, which is also really awesome."

"Cool," Carol said. "I started writing my first book. It's not great yet, but it's a start."

"Carol, that's fantastic," David said. "Really, I'm happy for you. Starting your first book is a big step."

"Yeah," Carol said. "It's terrifying, exciting and nerve wracking all at the same time."

"Well I'm sure that the final product will be fantastic," David said.

"Thank you," Carol said. "I'm sure that someday your first book will be as well."

They walked silently for a few minutes after that, not sure what to say to each other. They passed the park where they had hung out for the first time and David broke the silence.

"We had a lot of great times," David said.

"Yeah," Carol said, taking in a deep breath. "We did."

"Do you think it's even possible to just ignore it all and start over," David asked.

"Honestly, no," Carol said. "But I think we can come to grips with the fact that we had a lot of great times together, great times that we will always share. Whether or not we can continue with our friendship like we would like to, we'll always have memories to keep us warm at night."

"I like that logic," David said. "Even if we don't end up being friends, I'd like to stay acquaintances. Keep in touch over the years, I mean."

"I think I'd like that," Carol said.

"This is nice," David said. "Just walking and talking. It's sad, but I think that if we *are* going to be friends, I think we should do this, just take walks. I honestly don't trust myself to be in a room alone with you without trying stuff."

"It is sad, but I agree," Carol said. "I don't want to lose you as a friend again, but it's apparent that we don't need to be together *all* the time anymore. Maybe we could just take a walk like this, every Thursday after school, clear our minds, talk writing."

"Alright," David said. "I like that idea."

They continued walking, speaking slightly, for the next half an hour, before they went their separate ways to their own houses.

Friday morning, Robert had called William and told him to meet him at a strip club in a nearby city that night, around seven o'clock. He had gone to work, more on edge than usual. He had admittedly never been to a strip club before and the only real information he had about them came from TV shows and movies.

His heart was banging in his chest all day, because he was nervous. Nervous about going to the strip club, nervous about who Robert had invited, but mostly, nervous about the fact that this still wasn't bothering Erica one bit. He was sure it was just some kind of a trick, and that she was actually really angry.

After work, William and Erica drove back home together. Around four thirty, Erica cooked them an early dinner before he left. He asked her one final time whether she was really okay about him going to the strip club, and she once again told him that she was fine with it. After dinner, still in disbelief, William walked to the bathroom and took a quick shower. At five thirty, he got in his car and began driving toward the strip club.

David's mouth, and eyes, were wide open. He had the ass of a girl swinging in his face and an erection in his pants. He was still not sure why he had been invited to Mr. Morrison's bachelor party, but right now he wasn't exactly in a position to ask questions.

"Close your mouth, kid," Robert said. "You're starting to drool. If you get any in my beer, you're dead."

"Sorry," David said, wiping his bottom lip. "Why am I here again?"

"William has told me that you're one of his favorite students," Robert said. "And between you and me, I'm really his only friend, so I didn't know who else to invite."

Robert had made David a fake ID, so that he could have at least one beer when William showed up. He said he'd take the fall if they got caught, so David didn't say anything.

William pulled into the driveway and saw Roberts' car. He pulled up beside Roberts' car and parked. He turned the ignition off and he got out of his car. He locked the door, put his keys in his pocket, and walked toward the door.

When he walked in, he began looking around for Robert. A woman, dressed in nothing but her bra and panties, asked him if she could help him.

"Yes," William said nervously. "I'm looking for my friend Robert-"

"He's over there," she said, pointing.

"But I didn't give you his last name," William said.

"Trust me," she said, rolling her eyes. "We know Robert here. Before he met Lilly, he came here every weekend."

"Ah," William said. "I'm not surprised. Thank you."

William looked in the direction that she had pointed and spotted Robert. He couldn't make out the guy sitting next to him. He saw that Robert was laughing and talking up a storm with whoever it was.

"Robert," William said as he approached.

"Hey," Robert said. "Have a seat!"

William took off his jacket and sat down. He turned to say something to Robert and came to a stop as his eyes met David's.

"David," William said.

"Hey, Mr. Morrison," David said.

"Alright," Robert said. "Now we can order up some drinks."

"Woah," William said. "Drinks? He's only a freshman! What the hell is he doing here?"

"Relax," Robert said. "It's fine. I didn't know who else to invite, but I knew that you had said that you were kind of close to him, so I called him up and invited him."

"I said 'no'," David said.

"But," Robert said. "I was persistent. Come on, I didn't want it to be just the two of us, I mean this is your *bachelor party*. It's a big night!"

William sat back in his seat.

"You know what," William said. "I think I could use a drink right about now."

"Coming right up," Robert said. "Julie, could we have a round of beer?"

About five minutes later, the woman who had helped William find Robert, came over with beer.

"I've got to see your I.D." she said to David.

Nervously, he pulled out the fake I.D. and handed it to Julie. She looked at it and smiled. She looked at Robert and glared. She handed the I.D. back to David and handed William and Robert their beer. Then she thought for a minute. She handed David his and bent over.

"I'll allow him to have *one*," she whispered in Robert's ear. "Then it's soda. Understand?"

He nodded yes and thanked her.

"Alright, now let's have a toast," Robert said. "To my best friend Robert, and to his loss of single life!"

They all clinked their beer bottles together and began to drink.

"I paid them a little extra to put on a little show for you, by the way," Robert said. "Hit it, girls."

Five girls came out onto the stage in front of them. Two of them had "William" written on their breasts. They came over and began doing a dance in front of William. He chugged the rest of his beer right there. He wanted to have a good time, but he couldn't stop thinking of David being there and how awfully awkward Monday morning was going to be.

One of the other girls had "David" written on her breasts and the other had "Robert" written on hers. They began giving David and Robert lap dances.

David immediately had an erection and was embarrassed. Sweat was pouring off of his forehead. His heart was racing and he was extremely nervous. But, embarrassed as he was, he didn't move his eyes from the breasts that were only inches from his face.

Robert looked over at David.

"Don't waste that beer," He said. "Isn't this awesome, buddy?"

David convulsed slightly and Robert got concerned.

"Hey, are you alright," Robert asked, leaning over toward David.

"Yeah," David said. "Where's the bathroom?"

"Oh," Robert said. "Oh, gross man. The bathroom's back by the door where we came in."

David's stripper walked backstage, chuckling. David set his beer down and bolted toward the bathroom.

Robert took David's beer, wiped off the top and chugged it.

Twenty minutes later, the girls had finished their dances. David, Robert and William were finally all relaxed. David was sipping a Pepsi that Julie had brought him.

"I know it started off to a rough start," Robert said. "I'm sorry."

"No, I'm sorry," William said. "I never said 'thank you'. This may not have been the *best* idea you ever had, but I'm actually having a good time."

"Good," Robert said. "What about you, David?"

"Yeah," David said. "It's alright."

"I vote that we just sit here, have a few more drinks and just talk for the rest of the time," William said, laughing.

"Good idea," Robert said. "So, David, William told me what happened between you and that girl. That sucks, man. But it's for the best."

"You really think so," David said.

"Yeah," Robert said. "I was single for a long time after high school. I only dated a few girls, but they weren't pretty. I mean, they were attractive, but I just mean, oh, you know what I mean. But now I'm with Lilly, and I've never been happier."

"What are you saying?" David said.

Robert rubbed his eyes. "How do you deal with these teenagers day in and day out," he asked William. "I *mean*, David, that love is a waiting game. You'll go through some rough relationships, but you'll find the right one eventually."

"The right one," William said. "Are you thinking what I think you're thinking?"

"Not yet," Robert said. "I haven't known her long enough for that. But let's just say that you got me thinking about my future."

"Well," William said. "Let me be the first to say congratulations for whenever it happens."

"Thanks, man," Robert said. "So do you understand, David?"

"Yeah," David said. "Thanks for the advice."

"No problem," Robert said. "I say we hang here for about another hour then we get out of here."

"Another good plan," William said. "How about you get that girl to bring us one more round of drinks?"

"Will do," Robert said.

Robert dropped David off around eleven thirty.

"Hey, kid," Robert said after David got out of the car.

"What," David said, turning around.

"Give me that fake I.D." Robert said.

"I almost forgot," David said, pulling it out of his pocket.

"Yeah, I bet," Robert said. "Thanks for coming tonight."

"Beats hanging out here," David said, nodding his head toward the house.

"Well," Robert said. "Goodbye. Will you be at the wedding?"

"Yeah," David said.

"Alright, see you then," Robert replied.

David shut the door and Robert drove off. David walked toward the house and walked inside quietly. Brenda was already in bed. David walked into his room and turned on his computer. He wrote for another hour before going to bed.

Erica was still up grading papers when William got home.

"How was it," she asked.

"Interesting," William replied. "You'll never guess in a million years who Robert invited."

"Who," Erica asked.

"No really," William said. "Guess."

Erica thought for a minute. "Your father?"

"Worse," William said. "He invited, ready for it? David."

Erica stopped grading papers and looked up.

"Like David and Carol David," Erica asked.

"He claims that I don't have any other friends, so he decided that David was close enough to me to invite," William said.

Erica burst out laughing.

"It's not really funny," William said. "But in case you're wondering, I did have a good time. After I got over the shock of the fact that I was getting a lap dance a few seats away from a student who I'm going to have to face on Monday, that is."

"I can't believe he invited David," Erica said, still laughing. "Didn't he know how old he was?"

"Oh, he knew," William said. "That's the best part. He made David a fake I.D."

"How did that go," Erica asked.

"The bartender allowed him to have one beer," William said.

"Wow," Erica said. Then she burst out laughing, even harder this time. "Does this mean that I get to invite Carol to my bachelorette party?"

"If you really want to, be my guest," William said, chuckling. "I'm gonna head to bed. I love you."

He leaned down and kissed Erica.

"I love you too," Erica said. "See you in the morning."

William had been right, Monday morning was awkward. Even though he had enjoyed his bachelor party, it didn't seem to matter. Just seeing David sitting in his seat, as regular as ever, made him feel a bit queasy. He sat down at his desk and waited for the morning announcements. He closed his eyes and looked down at his desk. He opened his eyes and picked up a pen. He jotted down a note. It had been a long process, but he had finally narrowed the publishers down to five. He wrote them all down, preparing for the final elimination process and looked up. He was only about half surprised when he noticed that David and Carol were sitting next to each other.

David and Carol were indeed sitting next to each other, but they were not speaking this morning. They were both lost in their own worlds, rapidly writing down notes for their own creations in notebooks. On occasion, one of them would look up in William's direction, confusion in their faces, and then look back down after having an 'aha' moment and continue writing notes.

Finally, morning announcements began, and William pulled out his notes for his first class and set them in a pile on his desk.

At lunch, David and Tim sat with Carol for the first time since David and Carol had become friends again.

"Sounds interesting," Tim said, laughing.

David had just relayed the bachelor party to him and Carol.

"That's one word for it," David said. "How are you today, Carol?"

"Great," Carol said. "I'm three chapters into my book."

"Fantastic," David said.

"My alien romance story is done," Tim said, reaching into his backpack. "Here, take it and read it tonight if you want. Let me know what you think."

"I definitely will," David said, taking the story from Tim.

Tim still felt awkward when he was around David and Carol. He wasn't sure how to act, or what to say to Carol. So he mostly jumped in when he could and talked to David. He wasn't sure how they could be friends after what happened. He had never been in love, and figured that was why he didn't understand. *Love is strange* he thought.

"David," Carol said. "This is weird."

"I agree," David said.

"So do I," Tim said. David and Carol looked at him quickly, almost as though he didn't have a right in the conversation at hand. "Sorry. I'm gonna go put my tray away."

Tim got up and walked toward the back of the cafeteria, where he would leave his tray.

"We keep doing this," Carol said. "But we aren't friends anymore. It's going to just keep hurting for us, especially me. I've been thinking a lot about it, and I can't hang out with someone who cheated on me, I just can't. I'm going to go to my next class, I'll talk to you later, or maybe not, I don't know."

She stood up and took her tray to the back of the cafeteria and left the room. Tim sat down next to David and threw his arm around him briefly, and then retracted it.

"What now," Tim asked.

"I guess she doesn't think we can be friends again," David said.

"I can't blame her," Tim said. David looked up at him, surprised. "I mean you're a great guy, my best friend, but love is strange, David. Not so strange in your case though, you cheated on her. It's not a huge deal, it happens, you were horny. But whether or not you blame it on hormones, it's a fact."

"Yeah," David said. "I guess we just weren't meant to be."

"That's such a generic thing to say," Tim said. "Do you really think that anyone is made for anyone else?"

"I don't know what to think," David said. "All I think is that I should get to my next class. "I'll talk to you later."

David stood up and walked out of the room, deep in thought.

"I guess I'll just take your tray up too," Tim said after him, but David barely heard him.

News had traveled through the small High School community and by the end of the day, everyone knew that David and Carol had *once again* called their friendship quits. William was not surprised, but on the ride home, Erica shared a much different opinion.

"I'm so shocked that they couldn't stay friends," Erica said, sadly looking out the window.

"You're an English teacher," William said. "You know how these things go. Weren't you the one who told me that cheating is inexcusable?"

"In the romantic genre, yes," Erica said. "But sometimes people in real life are stupid enough to forgive and forget about that situation."

"I'm confused," William said.

"Well," Erica said, smiling. "It's like you said. They're stupid teenagers, *just* stupid enough, by the way, to forgive and forget about what David did to her."

They both burst out laughing in the car.

"It's nice to see that my darling shares the reality side of humanity that I have," William joked.

"I may not be a one hundred percent realist," Erica said. "But some things are common sense."

The next morning, William walked slowly into class. He hadn't yet even began his coffee, which was in a cup that he was holding in his right hand. Needless to say, he wasn't in a very good mood. He planted himself in his chair and forced his eyes open. His eyes closed for a moment, and he took a sip of his coffee, listening to his classroom.

"I'm sorry," Carol said. "I guess I was wrong. When I got home last night, I cried so hard because of what I had told you. I want to be your friend again."

William spat his hot coffee all over his desk.

"Are you fucking kidding me," he yelled.

"William," Erica said, running into his room. "It's alright."

"No, Erica, it's not," William yelled. "These goddamn kids need a dose of reality! It's a back and forth game with them. They need to learn to move on with their lives, date other people, have other heart breaks, like normal people!"

David and Carol, as well as the other students, were now wide eyed and looking straight ahead at their homeroom teacher. Other students, as well as faculty members, had gathered around the door.

"William," a voice said. "May I see you in my office, *right now?*"

William turned slowly, and saw Jodi standing next to Erica. He nodded 'yes' and he and Erica followed her out and down to her office.

"What the *hell* was that all about," Jodi asked, not impressed. "I've been a principal for fifteen years and I've never even *heard* of a display like that."

"I overreacted a bit," William said.

"A bit-" Jodi started.

"But," William said sternly. "I want to make it up to you, and to David and Carol. I believe that what I was saying was correct, though the way I said it was not acceptable. I have an idea. With your permission, as well as their parents', I want to invite the two of them to my house for the weekend. Both of them. I think it would be good for them to see how a, dare I say *normal,* and functional relationship works."

"I grant you that," Jodi said, rubbing her forehead. "They need it. I'll contact their parents today, and let you know at the end of the day what they say."

"Thank you," William said.

"Oh, you're free to go," Jodi said.

William and Erica stood up and walked out of Jodi's office. They walked back to their classrooms, said goodbye and went inside. First period had begun, but William just sat down in his chair.

"Um," William said, thinking quickly. "Just write about something that happened last weekend."

David smirked.

"Anything you want," William said, smiling in his general weekend.

William picked up the remainder of his coffee and chugged down two big gulps. Then he sat back in his chair and closed his eyes, trying to wake up.

William hadn't heard back from Jodi until Thursday morning, which was alright. She said that everything was set up. She said that Carol's mother had taken a bit of persuasion, but she had finally agreed. She had told Jodi that she was sick and tired of the charade that her daughter and David were putting her and everyone else through and that it needed to stop.

William asked Carol and David to step into the hallway with him and he motioned through Erica's classroom door for her to join them.

"Okay," William said. "First, I'd like to formally say 'I'm sorry' for the way I acted on Tuesday. I should have said that as soon as I got back to the classroom, but I was waiting for some news, and now I've gotten it." He stopped thoughtfully. He seemed to be looking for the right words. "I, Erica and I want you two to come to our house tomorrow afternoon and stay the weekend with us."

"Are you serious," David asked, obviously trying not to smile.

"This isn't funny, David," William said.

"Is this legal," Carol asked.

"We have your parents consent, so yes, it's legal," William said. "Erica, honey, you know what I want to say. I don't think I can say it without losing my temper again. Sorry, but would you mind?"

"Well, first of all, although we have your parents permission, you can both obviously say 'no' if you'd like to, but I really wish you would take our offer," Erica said. "You can't keep doing this to yourselves. When I had you spend that month a part, I thought that would cure this, your stupidity, I mean."

Carol's jaw dropped in disgust. "Stupidity? I'll have you know-"

"Carol, stop," Erica said. "Just stop. I thought, that by spending a month apart, you two would stop doing this. I figured that you would find new friends, interests, enjoy having time to yourselves, from what I've heard, I was right, but from what I've *seen* I guess that I wasn't as right as I'd hoped."

"You're only hurting yourselves," William said. "Quite honestly, have you really stopped to think about that?" William paused for a response. "I didn't think so. So please, take our invitation. Come stay with us for the weekend. If, after the weekend, you still want to be friends, together, or whatever it is that you two have, then so be it."

"I accept," David said, staring at the floor.

"So do I," Carol said angrily. "I guess."

Carol stormed off, and David looked her way, then back to William.

"I'm going back into the classroom," he said, turning around.

"I hope this is a good idea," William said to Erica.

"It is," Erica said. "Trust me."

David got back home and turned on his computer. He was about to write, when it hit him that he would be at Mr. Morrison's house all weekend, with his fiance and Carol. He wasn't sure why they wanted them to be there, but he knew Mr. Morrison well enough to know that there was a very good reason for it. He decided that there wouldn't be any problems, cast away the thought, and began writing.

Carol wasn't as easily convinced that it was a good idea.

"Why the hell did you agree to this," Carol yelled at Alice when she got home.

"You and David need to figure out just what you are, whether that is friends, boyfriend and girlfriend, or nothing at all," Alice said, trying to be calm but slightly yelling at the same time. "A weekend together is a fantastic place to figure that out. Honey, it's for the best. I'm sick of watching you two go back and forth with no solution. Don't do this because I am telling you to. Do it for yourself!"

Carol nodded, but she was still scowling. She turned and stormed away to her room and slammed the door.

By the next morning, Carol had thought it over and was convinced. She smiled at David and sat down next to him.

"I have a couple of movies in my backpack," she said. "In case Mr. Morrison and Erica go to bed early."

"Cool," David said.

He began to sweat slightly at that thought. The thought of him and Carol being up alone at night made him nervous, but he didn't let it show. There was a two minute pause, and then David spoke up.

"I hope this weekend works," David said. "Fixing whatever problems we have."

"Yeah," Carol said. "Me too."

The day went by quickly, and before they knew it, the final bell rang. David and Carol went to their lockers and got their things. They each had their school backpacks, as well as a larger travel bag in which they had put the clothes, toothbrushes and anything else they would need for the weekend.

They took their things back to Mr. Morrison's room and sat down, waiting for him.

"I'll just be a few minutes," William said. "I've got to finish typing this college recommendation letter for a Senior student, and I'll be ready to go."

He finished typing, and hit 'print'.

"As soon as I get those, we can leave," William said.

He realized that he kept contradicting himself, saying that they could leave when he got done. He realized that he was used to doing any of his after school things on his own, with no one waiting for him. Erica and him rode home together, but usually, they took things at their own pace and left when they were both ready. Today, however, he felt rushed to get things done quickly.

He returned to his room and put the three copies of the letter that he had printed out into his bag.

"Hold on," he said. "I just have to write myself a reminder so that I will remember to give these to him tomorrow."

He wrote on a sticky note and stuck it to the middle of his desk. Then he shut down his computer. He picked up his bag and walked toward the door.

"Alright, I'm ready," William said. "Just let me go see if Erica's ready."

Erica met him at the door, her bag in hand.

"I'm ready to go," Erica said.

The four of them began walking down the long hallway to the lobby.

"How was your day, dear," William said to Erica.

"It was fine," Erica said. "Billy Durante failed another test. If he doesn't up his game I'm going to have to fail him, and I really don't want to do that."

"Failing is never a fun thing to have to do," William said. "But it's necessary sometimes."

David and Carol shot each other looks, both amazed that this is what their teachers talked about in their free time. Neither David or Carol understood why anyone would want to talk about such a boring subject.

They all got to William's car and climbed in, William and Erica in front and David and Carol in the back.

"Okay," William said, starting his car. "Are you guys ready for this weekend?"

"Yeah," David said enthusiastically.

"I guess so," Carol said, not so enthused. "I hope it helps."

CHAPTER 14

William turned right, into his and Erica's driveway. He parked the car and turned off the engine. He opened the door and got out.

"Here we go," Carol said under her breath.

"What," David said to her.

"Nothing," Carol said back, opening up her door.

David and Carol followed William and Erica inside. They all took off their coats and hung them up. Then they took their shoes off and left them by the door. William and Erica began walking and David and Carol followed them, into the living room. Erica motioned for David and Carol to sit down on the couch, and they did.

"Okay," William said. "We just want to say a few things and then the weekend is yours. First, you must both finish all of your weekend homework before tomorrow morning. I'm just kidding."

David and Carol both chuckled nervously.

"But seriously," Erica said. "First, don't call us Mr. and Miss this weekend, our names *are* William and Erica, and this is our home. There's no need for the whole 'Mr.' and 'Miss' crap here."

"That's right," William said. "Now, why have we brought you here? You can't keep doing what you've been doing, but we've established that. Erica and I may not be the perfect couple, no one is, however, we are functional. You two seem to have a problem in that department. I can't force you, so I want to say that I *invite* you, to observe Erica and My daily lives as they are on the weekends."

"We're also here for you, in case you need to talk or have any urges this weekend," Erica said. "Don't give into any of those urges, instead, find whichever of us are nearest, day or night, and we'll help. This weekend will act as a romance boot camp of sorts, but I want you to have fun as well. Watch TV, whatever movies we have, eat what food you want, our house is your house for the next two days."

"And on Monday morning," William said. "And this is important, I want an official answer. I want to know whether or not you two are going to be friends, aren't going to be friends, whether you are going to be in a relationship, or whether you're not going to be in a relationship. That's what this is all about. You need to figure that out or it's just going to keep eating you up inside, trust me."

"That's it," Erica said, clapping her hands together. "That's our speech. The rest of the weekend, we're all going to go our ways and do whatever we need to do. Now, the sleeping situation. We have one spare bedroom, which one of you can take. The other can have the couch. What's it going to be?"

"I'll take the couch," David said.

"Okay," Erica said. "There's a space between the chair and couch where you can keep your things. Carol, come with me and I'll take you to your bedroom."

Carol followed Erica out of the living room and down a short hallway. At the end of the hallway was a bathroom. Erica opened up a door and held out her hand, leading Carol inside.

"I know it's not much," Erica said. "But it's our spare."

"It's perfect," Carol said. "I'm going to get my things set up if you don't mind."

"Okay," Erica said, turning around. "If you need us for any reason, our room is right down the hall."

She walked out of the room and closed the door behind her.

Carol smiled, looking at the small room. There was a single window that showed the small backyard. She sat her bags down in the corner. She sat down on the bed, which actually took up most of the room because of its size. She took a deep breath, preparing herself for the weekend. She stood up, realizing she had no reason for still being in here, and she walked over to the door. She walked out and went back out to the living room. She sat down on the couch, next to David, who hadn't moved.

"What do you want for supper," Erica asked David and Carol.

"I don't know," they said, at almost the same time.

"Never heard of it," William said. "How much does it cost?"

David and Carol both looked at William, confused.

"It was a joke," William said.

"How about pizza," Erica said.

"Sounds good to me," William said.

David and Carol both nodded 'yes'.

"Great," Erica said. "I'll call and order it and I can go pick it up when it's ready."

Erica called and ordered the pizza around four thirty.

"I'm going to leave to go get it in about ten minutes, does anyone want to go with me," she asked.

"I'll go," Carol said.

"Okay," Erica said. "Cool."

Ten minutes later, Erica was ready and putting on her shoes. Carol ran over and sat down, putting her shoes on as well. When they were done, they said 'goodbye' to William and David and headed out to the car.

"I'm going to my office to get some writing done," William said. "Feel free to watch TV if you'd like."

"Okay," David said. William walked off, notebook in hand and David grabbed the remote and turned on the TV.

"So how's school going," Erica asked Carol once they were on the road.

"It's going well," Carol said. "I'm passing everything."

"That's good enough then," Erica said, laughing. "When I was in high school, that's all that mattered to me. I would have preferred to spend the days reading if they had let me."

"Yeah, me too," Carol said with a chuckle. "Well that, and, never mind."

"I don't mean to pry, but why is it so tough," Erica said. "I was never cheated on, but I did have a guy break my heart in high school. And I never spoke to him again. And before you ask, yes, he was my first boyfriend."

"I don't know why it's so hard," Carol said. "It's childish really, and I know that. There's just something about him."

"Carol," Erica said. "Where's your father?"

"You're not the first person to ask if he's the reason that I keep going back to David, if he abused me," Carol said. "But the answer is 'no'. I've never met him."

"I'm sorry," Erica said. "I just-"

"I know," Carol said. "And I am thankful for all that you've done for me, I really am. I don't want to do this to myself, it's weird. It's like I'm addicted to a drug. I know it's bad for me, not to mention dangerous, and *stupid,* but I can't stop. I've tried."

"That's what this weekend is all about," Erica said. "We want to help you figure it out. Figure out why you're so addicted, as you put it. My question is 'why David'? Haven't you ever been interested in another guy?"

"Yeah," Carol said. "Not long ago, I dated a guy named Sean that I met at the mall. He was a nice guy, but there was just something that wasn't right. I can't explain it. Just a feeling he gave me. So I broke up with him. Then I was back at school the next day, and David was there, and I became addicted once again. I guess I just need to figure out what it is that keeps drawing me back to him. I'll tell you what, I'll think about it tonight and get back to you in the morning."

"It's a deal," Erica said, smiling. She pulled into the driveway of the store and shut off the ignition. Erica and Carol got out and walked inside to get the pizza.

When they got back to the house, they carried in the pizza and went into the kitchen. Erica got them each a plate and they each got two pieces and sat down at the table.

"Delicious," William said after swallowing his first bite. "There's Pepsi in the refrigerator if you want some."

David and Carol both stood up and walked over to the cupboard, where they each got a cup. David opened up the refrigerator and pulled out the bottle of Pepsi.

"Here," David said to Carol. "Let me pour it for you."

David took her cup and set it on the counter. He took off the top of the bottle and poured some into her cup.

"Thank you," Carol said, smiling.

"No problem," David said, smiling back.

Carol walked back over to the table and sat down, while David poured himself some Pepsi. David put the Pepsi away and walked back to the table, Pepsi in hand. He sat down and began eating his pizza.

"Thank you for the pizza," Carol said.

"No problem," William said, shrugging his shoulders. "Like I said, this weekend, our house is your house."

They finished eating in less than twenty minutes and they gathered once again in the living room.

William looked at his watch.

"Wow," William said. "It's only nine thirty, but I'm ready for bed."

"Me too," Erica said, fake yawning. "Let's head in."

They stood up and held hands.

"Goodnight," Erica said to David and Carol, but looking at Carol.

"Goodnight," David and Carol said.

"Goodnight," William said. "Stay up as late as you want, just be sure to shut the lights off before you go to bed. See you in the morning."

"That's the plan," David said, smiling.

Laughing, William turned around and he and Erica walked to their room.

"I know you're here to let them have time to themselves," William said. "But you should know that I really am tired."

"That's fine," Erica said. "I think I can handle getting to sleep just once without sex."

"Are you sure," William said, winking.

"Well, it's gonna be tough," Erica said with a smile. "But I'll be alright. Rest up, tomorrow night might be different."

They smiled at each other. William leaned over and kissed Erica. Then he laid down and fell asleep.

David and Carol sat together on the couch, watching TV.

"So," Carol said, trying to think of something to say. "How's Tim?"

"He's good," David said. "I think he's a bit confused about us being here this weekend."

"Yeah, it is a bit odd," Carol said.

"There's that," David said. "And the fact that there's a new science fiction movie in theaters he wanted to go see this weekend."

"Ah," Carol said. "I see. How long do you think you'll be up?"

"I don't really know," David said. "Probably about another hour. Pretty soon I'm going to stop watching TV and get some writing done so you can watch whatever you want."

"That's fine," Carol said. "I'll probably go to bed after this show."

"Okay," David said.

Five minutes of silence later, the TV show was over and Carol stood up. She stretched a bit and then turned to David.

"I'm gonna head to bed," Carol said. "I'll see you tomorrow."

"See you tomorrow," David said, as he shut off the TV.

Carol turned and walked down the hallway to her room. She grabbed her toothbrush and toothpaste out of her bag and walked to the bathroom. She put some toothpaste on her toothbrush and brushed her teeth quickly. She rinsed her mouth out and spat into the sink.

She walked back down the hallway to her room and opened the door. She walked inside and put her toothbrush and toothpaste on a stand next to the bed.

She yawned, then took off her shirt, throwing it into the corner. She pulled off her socks and threw them toward her shirt. Finally, she unzipped, then unbuttoned her jeans and threw them toward the rest of her clothes. She turned off the light and got into bed, pulling the blanket over her.

Then she began to think. She had promised Erica that she would. She tried her hardest to think of what it was about David that kept drawing her back to him. She was attracted to him, but she figured it had to be something more than that. She thought of him cheating on her. That should have sealed the deal, but it hadn't. She had still wanted to be with him, but why? Try as she might, she didn't have an answer. She hoped that she would have an answer by the end of the weekend. She continued to ponder the question, but before she had an answer, she fell into a deep sleep.

David was awoken Saturday morning to the sound of someone walking through the living room. He opened his eyes and saw William sluggishly walking into the kitchen, stretching as he walked.

David sat up and rubbed his eyes. He sat against the back cushions of the couch and tried to keep himself awake. He heard the coffee maker turn on and then William coming back toward the living room.

"David," William said quietly. "Sorry I woke you."

"It's fine," David said.

"I'm making coffee," William said. "When it's done, you're welcome to have some."

"Thank you," David said, stretching in his seat. "So, what do teachers do on Saturday?"

"Grade papers," William said, smiling. "I try to start as early as I can on Saturday, and if I'm lucky, I get to have a relaxing Sunday."

"How often do you get lucky," David asked.

"Every weekend," William said. "I'm going to let you in on a little secret. It's not about reading every little detail in every single paper, it's about knowing whose paper you're grading."

David nodded his head. "So about how long does it usually take you to grade all of the papers?"

"That all depends on how many details I feel like looking at on that day," William said.

David smiled.

"Let's go check on that coffee," William said, standing up and walking toward the kitchen. David stood up and followed him.

The coffee was just finishing when they walked into the kitchen. William poured them each a cup and turned to David, handing him his.

"Cream and sugar is in the cupboard if you want any," William said.

"No, I'm fine," David said.

They both over to the kitchen table and sat down across from each other.

"Did you sleep well," William asked.

"Yes," David said.

"Glad to hear it," William said. "What are your plans for the day?"

"I don't know," David said. "Getting some writing done probably."

"Good plan," William said. "That should keep you out of trouble."

Carol opened her eyes and looked up at the ceiling. It took her a moment to register where she was. She was so comfortable that she didn't want to get out of bed. The bed was like a cloud. She told herself to get up, but she somehow couldn't. It was as though the comfort was overpowering her will to get up. Finally, she came to the conclusion that she was hungry, something that even comfort couldn't even overpower.

She sat up in bed and threw her legs over the side. She opened her eyes wider, then shut them. She rubbed them and then proceeded to stand up. She walked over to the corner and got the clothes she had wore the previous day and put them on. Then she got into her duffel bag and pulled out a new outfit. She also grabbed her shampoo and body wash.

She opened the door and walked down the hallway to the bathroom. She pulled yesterdays clothes back off and turned on the water. She adjusted the water to the perfect temperature and turned on the shower.

William and David had heard Carol come out of her room and go down the hallway.

"Will you answer me an honest question," William asked David.

"Yes," David replied.

"How hard is it on you," William asked. "You know, being forced to be with her for a weekend."

"I think it's harder on her than it is on me," David said.

"That's not an answer," William said.

"I know," David said. "It's not that hard. You know, it's not *being* here with her, it's more the trying to figure out how, and why, it came to this."

"You don't know," William said, somewhat confused.

"I don't know why we're still trying to be friends," David said. "I'm to the point where I think I'd be comfortable just moving on with my life."

"That's good," William said. "That's just the answer I was looking for."

He finished up his cup of coffee and looked over at the coffee pot, as though he were pondering whether or not to have another cup.

"Well," William said. "I suppose I've got to get started on grading those papers."

David could tell by the look on his face, that William was actually talking about grading papers this time.

"Good luck," David said after William left the room.

"I'll need it," William said, turning around. He winked at David and turned back around, heading for his office.

Erica came out of their room just as William was going into his office.

"Good morning," she said as she passed his office door.

"Morning," he replied.

Erica made her way through the living room and into the kitchen. She didn't seem to notice David at first, not until she poured herself a cup of coffee and turned back around.

"David," she said. "Good morning."

"Good morning," David said, sipping his coffee.

"You're up early," Erica said, looking at the clock and seeing that it was nine o'clock. "Early for someone your age, I mean."

"William woke me up when he came through the living room," David said. "But it's okay."

"Did he say what he's going to be doing today," Erica asked.

"He said grading," David said.

"A teachers' work is never done," Erica said, taking her coffee and walking down the hall.

David sat at the table, planning out his day as he drank his coffee.

"William," Erica said, stepping into his office and closing the door. "I thought we agreed that we were going to each engage one of them into an activity that would get them away from each other."

"When did we say that," William said.

"Yesterday," Erica said. "On the way to work."

"Well I've got to get these papers graded," William said. "I only have ten to grade today, so I should be done in no time. Then I can come up with something to do."

"Alright," Erica said. "Take your time."

She walked over and opened the door. She stepped out into the hallway and saw that Carol was coming out of the bathroom.

"Good morning," Erica said. "We've got some coffee if you'd like some."

"I'm alright," Carol said. "Showers always wake me up in the morning."

"Must be nice," Erica mumbled, turning and walking back out to the kitchen table, her cup of coffee clutched in her hand.

At eleven o'clock, David went to the cupboard and pulled out bread and peanut butter. He got a knife from the silverware drawer and made himself a sandwich. He walked over to the kitchen table and quickly ate the sandwich. He walked to the fridge and got out a gallon of milk and poured himself a small glass. He quickly drank down the milk, washing down the dryness left by the peanut butter.

"Hey," a voice said from behind him.

David turned around and saw William.

"Hey, how's grading going," David asked.

"I'm done," William said, smiling. "Record time."

"Nice," David said. "I just had lunch."

"Cool," William said. "Where are Erica and Carol?"

"They said they were going to the store to get supper," David said.

"Oh, I see," William said. He was trying to think of something that the two of them could do together that would keep David's mind off of Carol. "Since I'm done early, do you want to do something, just the two of us since we're the only ones here?"

It sounded pretty creepy, even to him, but he couldn't think of anything else to say to get the ball rolling.

"Yeah," David said. "Sure."

"Like what," William asked.

"I don't really know," David said. "You asked."

"Good point," William said. "Look, I'm going to level with you, it'll be easier that way. Erica wanted us to each take this day and take you and Carol away from each other and do something that would distract your mind from each other. But I'm at a loss, I have no idea what to do."

"Do you like movies," David asked. "I mean, we could go see a movie. Just a thought."

"That's a good idea," William said, chuckling. "Because I can't, for the life of me, think of anything else. Let me get a sandwich and we'll head out."

Ten minutes later, they were headed out to the car. They got into the car and put on their seat belts. William turned on the ignition and pulled out of the driveway. The movie theater was about twenty minutes away, and he turned on the radio to fill the silence.

"So," William said. "How's your weekend going so far, David?"

"It's going well," David said. "You have a very nice house."

"Thank you," William said. "So, have you done any thinking about Carol yet?"

"No," David said. "But I will, I'm sure of it."

"Alright," William said. "Just remember what I said."

They pulled into the driveway to the movie theater and parked. They got out and drove to the front door and saw what was playing.

"What's it about, do you know?" William asked.

"Yeah," David said. "It's a mind numbing action film."

"Perfect," William said, opening the door and holding it for David.

They waited in line for about five minutes and got their tickets.

"Do you want any popcorn," William asked David, suddenly noticing how strange it must have looked seeing a teacher and student at the movies together. In a town this small, word got around quickly. William hoped that the purpose of he and Erica taking David and Carol to their house for the weekend had made its way around.

"Yeah," David said. "And a small Pepsi please."

"A large popcorn and two small Pepsi's," William told the man at the counter.

The man got their popcorn and drinks and William paid for them as well as their two tickets.

William handed David his Pepsi and popcorn and they walked into the theater and sat down, midway to the screen.

"I don't know when the last time I came to the movies when it wasn't on a date," William said, smiling. "To that same effect, I don't know when the last time I saw a mind numbing action film was either. It was probably college."

"That's a shame," David said, smiling.

"I know," William said. "It's top notch quality entertainment. Nothing like those dramatic academy award winners."

They looked at each other and burst out laughing. The theater darkened as the film began and they sat back and relaxed, ready to rid themselves from the troubles of the world for an hour and a half.

Erica and Carol had gone to a nearby city to go shopping. They had told David that they were going to get dinner, which wasn't entirely a lie. They were going to pick it up on the way home, after spending the day at the mall.

"So," Erica said. "This is where you met Sean?"

"Yeah," Carol said. "Over there on that bench. I was just people watching, studying for a story I was writing."

"Interesting," Erica said. "Oh well, if it wasn't meant to be, it wasn't meant to be."

"Yeah," Carol said, seeming to zone out in thought.

"You know what I haven't done since college," Erica said quickly, bringing Carol back into reality."

"What," Carol asked.

"Just tried on clothes with literately no intention of buying them," Erica responded, walking toward a nearby clothing store.

"Okay," Carol said, following quickly behind her.

They walked into the store and were immediately hit hard with the smell of strong perfume.

"Would you like to sample some perfume," asked a twenty-something year old girl, who was *way* too happy with her job.

"I think I already am," Erica choked.

She tried to take a deep breath and continued passed the girl.

"Okay," Erica told Carol. "I'll go this way, you go that way. Pick out a bunch of clothes. Meet me back here in five minutes and we'll go try them on."

Erica and Carol went their separate ways and began picking out a random assortment of clothes, bright, dark and everything in between. Carol was barely even paying attention to what she was grabbing. She was so infatuated with what she was doing, that style didn't matter for the first time in her life.

Erica was filled with an adrenaline she hadn't felt in years.

They met back at the place they had began and, without even looking at each others' clothes, they walked toward the dressing rooms.

"Okay," Erica said. "Let's flip a coin to see who goes first." She pulled out a quarter and flipped it into the air. "Heads."

The coin landed on tails and she frowned, then smiled.

"You're up," Erica said to Carol.

Carol stepped into a dressing room, and hung her chosen clothes up. She took off her shirt and pants and folded them up behind her. She chose to try on a bright yellow dress first and pulled it on. She laughed at how ridiculous she looked in such a bright dress but didn't care. This adrenaline rush wasn't going anywhere anytime soon. She opened up the door and stepped out.

"That's....bright," Erica said, forcing a smile. Her and Carol both began laughing.

Carol walked back inside and changed into a long, tan coat that looked like something a detective would wear.

She stepped back out and Erica's eyes grew wide.

"Wow," Erica said. "I know you're not going to agree, but that's *you*."

"Get out," Carol said.

"No, I'm serious," Erica said. "You look great in it!"

"I'll keep that in mind," Carol said, looking down at the coat. She looked back up. "I only have one more thing left that I picked out."

She stepped back inside and put on another dress, this one a long blue dress. She stepped out again and Erica looked at her in disgust.

"I know," Carol whispered. "But I just can't believe they sell something that looks like this."

Erica laughed again and stood up. "Okay, go change back into your clothes. It's my turn!"

Carol turned around and walked back inside. She changed back into her clothes.

She walked out and Erica practically ran her over trying to get into the dressing room.

"I only have two," Erica said from behind the door.

Inside, Erica pulled off her shirt and pants and put on a purple dress and came back out.

"That looks really nice on you," Carol said.

"Thank you," Erica said. "The next one won't."

"Then why are you trying it on?" Carol asked, smiling.

"Trust me," Erica said.

She went back into the changing room and pulled over her head a long, vomit colored dress and opened the door again.

"That's disgusting," Carol said.

Erica bent down, doing her best not to rip the dress. "It costs...ready for this, five hundred dollars."

"What," Carol exclaimed. "That's ridiculous."

"It's the most expensive thing in here," Erica said. "I just wanted to say I've worn it."

They laughed as Erica walked back into the changing room and changed back into her clothes.

The movie ended and William and David stood up. David held the popcorn bag up and let the last tiny pieces of the popcorn fall into his mouth. He swallowed them and they walked out of the theater.

"That was nice," William said. "Meaningless violence and blood from left to right. A true guy movie."

"It was definitely better than I thought it would be," David said.

"Me too," William said, smirking. "But that's not saying much."

They threw away the popcorn bag and sodas and they walked through the lobby of the movie theater and outside to the parking lot. They got into the car and put on their seat belts.

"Let's go out for dinner," William said.

"Erica said that she was going to buy dinner," David said.

"I know," William said. "But I'm hungry now. Let's go to a steak house."

"Alright," David said. "It's been a long time since I had a good steak."

"Then it's settled," William said firmly. "We shall go eat steak."

The closest steak house was only about five minutes away. William drove there and parked the car. He and David got out of the car and walked inside.

They sat down at a table and a waitress came over and handed them each menus.

"Can I get you some drinks to start with," she asked.

They both ordered Pepsi's and began looking at the menu. A minute later, the waitress returned with their drinks.

"Are you ready to order," the waitress said.

"Yes," William said. "I'll have a medium rare steak."

"I'll have the same," David said.

"Alright," the waitress said, walking away.

William took in a deep breath.

"You don't get a smell like that at some crappy fast food restaurant," William said

"You've got that right," David said, also taking a deep breath in.

"This has been a nice day," William admitted, looking down at the table. "I don't get out much anymore. And if I do, it's just to take Erica to a doctor's appointment to see how the baby's doing."

"I've had a good day as well," David said. "I never thought that a day out spent with a teacher would actually be enjoyable, no offense."

"None taken," William said. "I have always felt the same about students."

William reclined in his seat and cracked his neck.

"You make me feel young, kid," William said, moving his eyes from the window to David. "That's what my father used to say whenever we had a day out, just the two of us."

"Glad to hear it," was all David could come up with to say back.

"Can you believe that the school year is only a couple of months away from being over," William said.

"No," David said. "It's crazy. I feel like my first day of high school was yesterday."

"So do I," William said, half smiling. "Time goes by faster and faster the older you get, David. Live every day moment to moment, not hour by hour. Before you know it, high school will be over, then college, then you'll have a job. And then things start to go by *really* fast."

For a few minutes, they were both silent. William stared thoughtfully out the window.

He thought of everything he had just told David. High school really did feel like it was only a few years ago. So did college. So did the three smaller jobs he had taken before his final teaching position. And now he was engaged and about to become a father. He reached for his Pepsi and took a long sip. He swallowed and looked up at David, who was looking in the direction of the kitchen.

Suddenly, the waitress emerged from the kitchen door with a tray that had two plates on it. She walked over and stopped at their table. She placed a plate in front of each of them and they said 'thank you'.

David was going to say something, but all that came out was a sound that was more of a groan than anything. He was literately drooling, but he didn't notice. He was too focused on the steak. He cut off a rather large piece and picked it up with his fork, shoving it into his mouth.

William laughed at the sight, and cut off a reasonable piece of his and put it into his mouth. They were enjoying their steak so much that they did not speak for the remainder of the meal.

Erica pulled into her and William's driveway and parked the car.

"I wonder where William is," she said.

They got out and walked inside, the bags of groceries in hand.

"David's not here either," Erica said.

"Maybe they got bored," Carol suggested.

"Maybe," Erica said.

"Well, there's no telling when they'll be home," Erica said. "Let's start making supper."

"Let's," Carol asked.

"Of course," Erica said. "Have you ever cooked before?"

"Nothing that can't be made in a microwave or put into a sandwich," Carol admitted.

"Well," Erica said. "An oven is similar to a microwave, except for the fact that it actually cooks the food."

She pulled out the chicken from a bag and pulled it from the package.

"Could you reach into that cupboard and get me a metal pan," Erica said.

Carol reached into the cupboard and got the pan.

"Here you go," Carol said.

"Thank you," Erica said.

Erica put the chicken into the pan and set the preheat timer on the oven.

"Alright, let's just let that preheat," Erica said, walking over to the kitchen table.

Carol followed her over and sat on the opposite side as Erica.

"So," Erica said, looking over to Carol. "We've had a fun day, huh?"

"Yeah we have," Carol exclaimed, smiling.

"Good," Erica said. "I'm glad. So did you have time last night to think about my question."

"Oh," Carol said. "Yeah, I think I have a pretty good answer."

"A pretty good answer," Erica chuckled. "Great, but is it a *true* answer, that's the real question."

"Yes, its true," Carol said.

"Good, glad to hear it," Erica said. "Let me hear it."

"David took my virginity, he was my first, and he was my first boyfriend," Carol said. "And as far as I know, it was the first time for him too. We're connected that way forever. We were each others firsts. And so, that's why I'm still attracted to him."

Erica looked down at the table thoughtfully. She stuck her tongue out slightly and licked her lips. Her tongue went back into her mouth and she looked up at Carol. She nodded.

"That *is* a good answer," she agreed. "Now you just have to figure out what to do about it. Like I told you, you're always going to have that feeling toward David somewhere in your heart, but you have to find that barrier. Either that, or you just have come to grips with the fact that you can't be friends with him. It's that simple. You don't want to be in another relationship with him, I know that. So you have to figure out if it's possible to have a friendship with him. And if not, then you just have to move on. It sounds harsh, but it's the truth."

The oven beeped and Erica stood up and walked over to it. She opened up the oven and put the chicken inside and closed it. She set the timer and walked back over to the table.

They heard a car turn into the driveway and looked outside to see William pulling into the driveway, David sitting in the passenger seat.

"There they are," Erica said. "I wonder if they've eaten yet."

William and Erica went to bed at nine o'clock, leaving David and Carol sitting in the living room alone.

"David," Carol said. "Do you ever think about us getting back together?"

"Woah," David exclaimed. "No segue or anything?"

"Sorry," Carol said, smiling. "It just came out."

"It's fine," David said. "The thought comes to me on occasion, but I've learned to ignore it. I've come to the conclusion that it's not the brightest idea that I could come up with."

"Okay," Carol said. "I agree with that. But on occasion, I get the same thought. I know we've both thought it before, but I wish we could just go back."

"We can't, though," David said. "It's okay. It's in the past, don't fight it. It will only make it worse. And as much as I'd like to think it's possible, I don't think we should hang out anymore.

It would be different if we had been friends *before* we started dating, but we weren't. We dated, had sex, had some fun times, but it's over. I'm sorry."

"It's fine," Carol said, tearing up. "I agree, I really do, but it just hurts."

David walked over and hugged her. He kissed her on the cheek and took a step back.

"I'm gonna go to bed," he said. "If you want to keep watching TV-"

"No, I'm going to go to bed too," Carol said. "I'll see you tomorrow. Goodnight."

Carol turned and walked down the hallway to the room and opened the door. She didn't turn on the lights. She didn't even take off her clothes. She found the bed and crawled in. She didn't sleep, she just laid there, her eyes staring at the dark ceiling.

In the living room, David was relieved. He took off his shirt and laid down on the couch. He drifted into sleep almost immediately, finally feeling the relaxation he had been needing for months.

Sunday morning, everyone slept in until ten thirty. Slowly, they got up and got ready. By eleven, they were all assembled in the kitchen, where William started making coffee.

"How did everyone sleep?" William asked, incoherently sitting down and grasping his coffee between his two hands.

Erica, Carol and David all muttered a "good" and then gathered around the coffee machine. Erica poured them each a cup of coffee and, as though in a trance, they followed each other over to the table, where they sat down.

They didn't say much until they had ingested their first cups of coffee. By the time the second pot had been made and William and Erica had their second cups, they were much more lively.

"Lunch," Erica blurted out as though she had suddenly had an epiphany. "Who wants lunch?"

"Sounds good," William said. "What are we going to eat?"

"Good question," Erica said. "I think we have peanut butter and jelly for sandwiches."

"Breakfast of champions," David said, standing up. "Where is everything? I'll make us each a sandwich."

"Bread and peanut butter are in the cupboard and jelly's in the refrigerator," Erica said." Thank you, David."

Less than five minutes later, David had made all four sandwiches and put them each on a plate and handed them to everyone.

"What do you all want to do after lunch," Erica asked.

"Take a nap," David suggested.

Everyone smiled and beginning to eat their sandwiches.

An hour later, William was in his office, getting some writing done, and David was in the living room doing the same. Erica and Carol were outside, sitting on the lawn, taking in some bright, warm sun. Carol told Erica about the short conversation that had taken place between her and David the night before.

"After, I went into the room and cried for about an hour," Carol said. "But then, I had the realization that he was right. It's really for the best. I just need to take a breath and move on with my life." Carol smiled at the thought of being able to finally be over everything with David. "Thank you, by the way, for being there for me and listening to me talk through all of this."

"It's no problem," Erica said. "I know that I'm a teacher, and that makes it hard to believe, but I was a teenage girl once myself. I know how hard it is. Some days it seems like it will never get better, but luckily, as you're learning now, it does, for the most part. You'll still be thinking about David when you're my age to an extent, but it won't be about how much you miss him. He'll just be a great memory you have from your younger days."

"That's a reassuring thought," Carol said.

She looked up, squinting her eyes at the brightness of the sun. She took in a long, deep breath and held it for five seconds. She let it go and closed her eyes. The future seemed so far away, but for the first time in months, she felt positive that the future wasn't going to be that bad. She was actually looking forward to it.

Monday morning, everyone was up by five thirty and in the car by six o'clock. William drove them all to Bucksport High. He had told David and Carol that they could leave their things in his trunk until the end of the day and get them later so they didn't have to worry about them. He pulled into the driveway of the school and parked the car. They all got out of the car and walked inside. They split into the classrooms and prepared for their days.

David and Carol sat on opposite sides of the room. William made a mental note that they hadn't spoken to each other all morning. They had barely even looked at each other, with the exception of when they were all sitting at the kitchen table together that morning.

He took a sip of his coffee. He set his travel mug down and smiled. They were no longer on or off. They were no longer wondering whether or not they would date again. Their interest in each other was completely gone now.

William smiled, leaned back in his chair and closed his eyes. He couldn't believe it. He had *wanted* to believe it, but he hadn't made any promises with himself about it. But he had been wrong. He had succeeded. The weekend had been a success.

CHAPTER 15

For David, nothing really changed after the weekend at William and Erica's house. He hung out with Tim, occasionally went to the movies, and wrote, just as he had. As he had told Carol that night, he had already come to grips with the fact that getting back together with her again was a mistake. That had already been a part of his life before that weekend. He was over her and it felt amazing.

"I'm really proud of you," Tim said one Thursday at lunch. "If we were old enough, I'd buy us some beer, but we're not."

David laughed and shook his head.

"But," Tim said, looking at David. "How about you come hang out with me this weekend at my house. My parents can pay for the pizza and soda for a change. That can be my gift to you."

"Using your parents as means to get a gift for a friend to show how proud you are of him," David said thoughtfully. "I like it."

The bell rang and they took their trays up and went their separate ways to their classes.1

Carol didn't have the same reaction. The weekend had taken a serious toll on her. She *did* agree that they shouldn't be together anymore, but the idea of not even being friends with David anymore wasn't so hot to her. She had agreed even with herself that they shouldn't date anymore, but she hadn't even toyed around with the idea of them not even being friends. Even with the obvious reasons floating through her head why they *shouldn't* be friends, it still hurt.

She breathed in the warm spring air as she slowly walked home, staring at the ground, lost in these thoughts and more.

Besides all of the thoughts of David, she was still trying to fathom the fact that it was now May, and that her Freshman year of high school was almost over. It had gone by so quick. She barely believed it some days unless she actually looked at a calender.

She remembered her teachers telling her and the other students at the end of her eighth grade year that high school would go by fast, but she hadn't really believed them. She figured that if the rest of her school years had gone by so slowly, why would high school be any different. But it was different. It was *very* different. As she turned into her driveway, she wished that she had listened to those teachers more closely and taken them a lot more seriously. The problem was that in eighth grade, the only thing that Carol had cared about was the fact that the school year was, once again, coming to an end and that she was about to be on summer vacation. She only wished that she felt that way now.

When she walked through the door, Alice was in the kitchen making a sandwich.

"Do you want one, Carol," Alice asked.

"No," Carol said. "I'm fine."

"Well you don't sound fine," Alice said, turning around. She stopped dead and her eyes widened. "And you certainly don't *look* fine."

"Gee, thanks, Mom," Carol said, sitting down at the kitchen table.

"You look like you've been crying," Alice said.

"You're very perceptive," Carol said quietly.

"Oh honey," Alice said. "I know it's hard. You have to remember, I've been there too. That's why I divorced your father, remember, because he cheated on me. I hadn't brought it up to you this whole time, because I knew that you were going through a lot."

"I know, Mom," Carol said. "I should have talked to you first, but, I don't know. I guess I just never really needed to talk when I was home. Mostly when I saw David. But I surely could use someone to talk to now."

"Okay," Alice said. "Let's do this, then. Let's have a girls' day on Saturday, huh? We can go out to lunch, then to a movie, sound good?"

"Yes," Carol said. "It sounds very good. I'm going to go to my room and write, I love you."

"Okay," Alice replied. "I love you too."

The next day, after school, David and Tim walked to David's house, where David packed a backpack for the weekend. Then they walked across town to Tim's house.

"Our Freshman year is almost over," Tim said in disbelief.

"I know," David said, watching the ground as he walked. "So much has happened in such a short amount of time. I had my first relationship, lost my virginity, met a great friend...."

David trailed off and Tim began to speak.

"Yeah," Tim said. "And I feel like I've grown as a writer. Do you feel that? I know that Middle School was only a year ago, but I feel like a changed writer. I mean, I'm still writing science fiction, but at least it's *good* science fiction."

"I definitely agree with you," David said. "That part of my life has changed a *lot*. But, I suppose that it has to do with life experience. The more we experience in our lives, the more we, as writers, have in our memory banks. The more situations we have to play around with and build characters and stories with."

They got to Tim's house and walked inside.

"You know, the crazy thing is that they say that the next three years will only go by quicker," Tim said.

"With the speed of tings lately, I believe it," David said. They walked into the living room and sat down on the couch.

"Mom and Dad went out for the evening tonight," Tim said. "They said they won't be back until later. They left us fifty dollars to use, they said in case we got bored and wanted to go to the movies."

"I'm actually good with hanging out here for the night and watching crappy TV shows," David laughed. "It's just been one of those weeks."

"I know what you mean," Tim said. "With finals coming up, there's so much more review and studying happening, even *in* school!"

"It's tiring, really," David said. "I wonder if this is the way it is in college."

"Oh, man," Tim said. "How can you even think that far ahead?"

"I don't know," David said. "I don't have any idea where I want to go, or what I want to major in, but I know that I want to go."

"That's good," Tim said. "It's good to have goals, in fact, let's set one right now. What time do you want to order the pizza?"

"Well, figuring the time of cooking and delivery, how about four thirty?" David said.

"It's a plan," Tim said, turning on the TV. "I don't even know what this show is, but I don't care. I'm too lazy to look for anything else."

The pizza got there at five o'clock and Tim paid the delivery man for it and then he took it inside. He put it on the coffee table in the living room and went to the kitchen.

"What do you want to drink," Tim hollered to David from the Kitchen.

"Pepsi's fine," David responded.

Tim poured them each a glass of Pepsi and walked back into the living room.

"Here you go," Tim said, handing David his Pepsi.

"Thank you," David said, taking his glass.

Tim opened up the box and pulled out a slice of pizza and took a bite. David did the same and they both stared at the TV.

"Okay," Tim said. "I'm tired of whatever this station is. What do you want to watch?"

"Whatever," David said. "Hit 'guide'. I'm sure we'll find something."

They found an old comedy show and watched it while they ate their pizza. It occurred to David that his and Tim's weekends together were really boring at times, but at least they were relaxing.

They stayed up until two in the morning, before they finally decided that they should go to bed.

Saturday morning, Alice woke Carol up at nine o'clock and told her that they were going out for breakfast, something they had not done in many months. Carol forced herself out of bed and pulled on her clothes. Within the half hour she had been awake, she had showered and was in the car with Alice, riding to the nearest diner.

Alice parked the car and they walked inside and sat down. The waitress came over and handed them menus.

"Hello," said the waitress. "Can I start you off with some coffee?"

"Yes, please," Carol said, still only about half coherent.

"I'll have some as well," Alice said, snickering. "Although I don't think I will need nearly as much as my daughter here."

"Okay," the waitress said, smiling. She poured them each some coffee and then looked up. "Are you ready to order or do you need some more time?"

"I'm ready," Alice said, looking over at Carol. "Do you need a minute, hon?"

"No," Carol said, glancing down at the menu. "I just spotted what I'm going to have."

"Okay," the waitress said, pulling out a pen and small notepad. "What will it be?"

"I'll have bacon, scrambled eggs and french toast," Alice said. "And I'll also have a glass of orange juice."

"Okay," the waitress said, jotting down the order.

"And I'll have the ham and cheese omelet with peppers and onions," Carol said. "And a glass of orange juice."

"I'll put those orders right in for you," the waitress said. Carol and Alice handed her their menus and she walked away.

"This is nice," Alice said. "I really wish we got to do this more often."

"So do I," Carol said. "It's nice, just the two of us hanging out."

"It really is," Alice said. "I don't know why, but I thought that these days were over when you turned thirteen. It's nice to know that there's at least *one* member of your generation who doesn't mind spending quality time with their parent."

"I don't mind," Carol said. "I have a feeling that today's going to be really fun. Just what the two of us need."

The waitress brought their meals fifteen minutes later and they began eating.

"This omelet is perfect," Carol said with a full mouth.

"So are these scrambled eggs," Alice said. She swallowed her eggs and looked up at Carol. "So how are things at school going? I know we don't get much time to talk about your school life anymore."

"Things are going well," Carol said. "I'm passing all of my classes."

"Passing," Alice said with a smile. "Now does that mean you're getting *good grades* in all of your classes?"

"Yes, Mom," Carol said with cadence.

"Well that's good," Alice said. "You're a better student than I was."

"Well, you graduated," Carol said.

"Take it from me," Alice said. "Anyone can graduate high school with little to no effort whatsoever. Do well in high school and you'll have a better chance of getting higher education. I graduated, yes, it's true. I *barely* graduated. My grades my senior year weren't exactly something to note. I did what I could to keep my grades above failure so that I could have more time to spend with my friends."

Carol silently pondered this as she and Alice both finished their breakfast and coffee. When they were done, Alice got the bill and paid for the meals.

They walked out to the car and got inside.

"Where do you want to go next," Alice asked. "It's ten thirty, so we still have the whole day ahead of us."

"No idea," Carol said. "Let's go window shop at the mall."

"Now, there's something I haven't done in a while," Alice said.

Alice drove to the mall, where they got out and walked around, eating free samples, looking for deals, and trying on clothes, as well as jewelry, that they would have only been able to afford if they won the lottery.

They spent four hours, slowly walking through the mall, its two floors and its thirty-five stores. They had lunch in the food court, at a sandwich shop that they found. After they decided that they had worn their welcome, as store clerks began looking at them angrily for not buying anything, they decided to leave the mall.

"It's only four now," Alice said. "Too early to quit yet. Want to go see a movie?"

"Yes," Carol said, thinking about how the last time she had gone to the movies with her mother must have been close to five years ago. "I'd love to."

They got back in the car and drove to the movie theater and got out. They walked inside and got into line. The movie playing that night was a new comedy film, a perfect end to the perfect mother and daughter outing.

Alice paid for their tickets, as well as their popcorn and sodas that they wanted, and they walked into the theater.

"Where do you want to sit," Alice asked.

"How about the middle," Carol said, pointing to a couple of seats.

They walked to the seats and sat down, placing their drinks into the cup holders.

"This is fun," Alice said. "This whole day has been fun. We should really try to do this more often."

"Definitely," Carol said. "I don't remember the last time I had this much fun. What are you doing next weekend?"

"This again," Alice said, smiling.

Carol smiled back as the lights went down. The movie began and they sat in the dark theater, as the trailers for the films to come began.

When the movie was over, they drove back to the house, where they ate a couple of sandwiches for supper, and then went to bed, both of them tired from the long, yet fun day they had both had.

Monday morning, William's home room was full of the sounds of stressed out teenagers talking, complaining really, about the finals they would soon be taking. They were complaining about the studying, which they most likely weren't doing anyway, and how much harder studying for finals was now that they were no longer in Middle School.

A couple of the students were having a private conversation about how unfair it was that the Seniors would soon be getting out, earlier than everyone else, just so that they could have their marching practice and graduate. William, hearing this, noted that these two students did not mention the fact that the Seniors had to do their finals also, or the fact that they had earned the right to end their years early.

This morning, for whatever reason, William had woken up earlier than early, and was much more awake than usual. He had gotten coffee, out of habit, but he hadn't needed it. He was naturally awake today, for whatever reason. He had enjoyed his dream the night before, where he had dreamed of the birth of his and Erica's child, who was a girl in the dream, and its growing up through the years, and even witnessing the child's own high school graduation before waking up.

David sat in class, with a science book, not a fiction book, opened up on his desk. Next to the book, there was an open notebook, which he was quickly jotting down notes from. The notes he was taking were for his biology exam, which was the only one that he was stressing about at all. Science had never been his strong suit, which was why he was slightly nervous about the exam. He was taking down notes on anything he didn't have completely memorized, which was unfortunately, most of the material in the book.

Carol sat at her desk, with a pile of books from English on her desk. She wasn't nervous about the exam, but she decided that it would be best if she at least reviewed the readings from the class. She was slowly skimming all of the books, plays and poems which she had read over the year. She took the occasional note, if there was something she wasn't too sure about.

The bell rang and Carol slid her books back into her backpack and stood up. She walked out of the classroom, passing David, who looked as though he needed a lot of sleep.

David groaned at the sound of the bell. He had only began to scratch the surface of his biology book, but he slid his notebook into the book, as a makeshift bookmark, and shoved the book into his backpack. He rubbed his eyes, stood up, and stepped out of the classroom. He walked down the hallway for about thirty seconds before he stopped dead, realizing that he had just left his first classroom.

As he walked back to William's classroom, he recalled how Carol had done the same thing on the first day of school. He made his way back to his seat, embarrassed, and sat down. He looked up at William, who was extremely cheerful for the morning.

"I just wanted to start today's class by giving you some encouragement," William said. "I know that you're all terrified about your finals, that's natural. You're doing everything you're supposed to be doing. You're nervous, not only for your first high school finals, but also for the fact that your first year of high school is coming to an end. You may not agree with me, but that's just because you don't realize it. Right now, the images of your upcoming summer vacation is all that you're thinking about. But, what I wanted to say is don't be nervous. High school exams aren't as hard as you think. That's not to say that you shouldn't study, but I think it's worth throwing out there that you shouldn't study to the point where you're passing out at two in the morning. You should pick a study technique that works for you, as well as one that will allow you to actually *remember* the materials you're studying. With that all being said, good luck with your final exams. Now, let's get to class."

When Mother's Day had rolled around and William and Erica had realized that they had been too busy to plan anything, they covered up their mistake by telling their mothers' that they were planning on doing a 'parent's day' celebration on Father's Day and that they would have them all over for dinner on that day.

The day before, William and Erica found themselves at the local supermarket, picking out two cards each for their mother and father. They also bought a bouquet of roses for each of their mothers and a bottle of red whine for the occasion. They also bought their father's each a new tool box at the local hardware store on the way home.

The next morning, they began to prepare a large turkey dinner. The dinner would resemble that of a Thanksgiving dinner, complete with mashed potatoes, gravy, stuffing, a few vegetables and cranberry sauce.

They began preparing the meal at ten o'clock in the morning, with their coffee cups still in hand. The preparation only took about an hour. They put the turkey in the oven at one o'clock. At three thirty, they began boiling the potatoes and stuffing. At three thirty, their parents' showed up and they were happy because, while the turkey was not finished, they had miscalculated the time that the rest of the food would take to cook and it was done.

"Let's eat now," William said. "We'll just have a hell of a desert!"

Everyone chuckled, grabbing plates and silverware. Everyone filled their plates and sat around the kitchen table. They ate and chatted, complimenting William and Erica on the food. At five o'clock, the turkey was finally finished and William pulled it out of the oven and set it out on the counter. He sliced it up into many different pieces and told everyone it was ready for their consumption.

"Sorry that the stuffing wasn't in the turkey," Erica said, slightly embarrassed. "I wasn't thinking."

"It's fine," said Mona. "The stuffing was still delicious and that's all that counts."

They all got a healthy helping of turkey and sat back down at their seats.

"So," William said. "How has everyone been?"

"We've all been great, I'm sure," said Stephen. "I'm mostly sure because *we four* call each other, unlike another couple I can mention."

Their four parents gave William and Erica a glare that seemed half serious. Right as William and Erica looked like they were going to burst into tears with some explanation, the four of them began laughing uncontrollably.

"The look on their faces," Kathleen exclaimed. "Priceless!"

"They thought you were serious," Carl exclaimed.

"It's good to know that I've still got it," Stephen said through his laughter. "Now seriously, how have you two been? How's that grandchild of ours?"

"The baby is doing fantastic," Erica said. "It's looking like it's going to be a very easy birth, well, I mean that the baby will be healthy."

"It won't be that bad, dear," Mona said.

"Yeah," Erica said. "That's what all mothers say."

"I've always said that it's for every woman to experience on her own," Kathleen said. "It's different for everyone."

"I can live with that," Erica said. "It's realistic."

"So," Mona said. "How are plans for the wedding going?"

"They're all done," Erica said.

"Oh no," Kathleen said. "They can't be. There's always something else to plan for a *wedding*!"

"No, really," Erica said. "We made the plans as fast as possible so that it would be less stressful. All that's left now is my bachelorette party."

The room went silent.

"What," Erica exclaimed, pointing at William. "*He* got a bachelor party!"

"When was this," yelled Stephen. "And *why* wasn't I invited?"

"It was nothing," William said. "A friend and I just went out."

"Oh, how nice," Kathleen said. "Out where?"

"To a, uh, club," William replied.

"A *strip* club," Kathleen asked furiously.

"Yeah," William said quietly.

"That's disgusting," she retorted. "You are getting *married*!"

"Actually, I was the one who got him to go," Erica said.

"Yeah," William said. "I didn't even want to go."

"What kind of a life do the two of you live," Kathleen asked.

"What do you mean you didn't want to go," Stephen said.

William had no response. He looked at Erica, trying his hardest to tell her with his eyes to change the subject. It took her a minute, but she finally picked up the signal.

"To our parents," Erica said, holding up her glass of wine. "And all of the love they showed us and all that they taught us. Cheers."

They all held up their glasses and repeated 'cheers'.

"It's getting late," William said.

"It's only seven," Kathleen replied.

"Yeah, but we have work tomorrow," William said quickly. "And we have papers to grade, so you all have to go now, goodbye."

Awkwardly, William and Erica's parents stood up and said their goodbyes, hugging and kissing their children and soon to be children in law. They all said a strangely nice goodbye to the baby inside of Erica's womb, and then they departed.

"No more family dinners," William said, half serious. "They all end with me having to ask our parents to leave early."

"I think it's funny," Erica said, sticking her tongue out at William and biting it with her teeth. "I think we should do this once a month."

She laughed loudly as she began picking up the dishes and taking them to the sink.

"You laugh," William said. "Next time you can be the one who tells them that they have to leave."

Lilly picked Erica up at nine o'clock. They stopped by Carol's house and she was waiting outside. Erica had only been half serious about inviting Carol to her bachelorette party, but after they bonded on the weekend that her and David had stayed over, she had considered it more seriously.

"Where are we going," Erica asked Lilly as they pulled away from Carol's driveway.

"It's a surprise, I told you," Lilly said.

"Surprises are for children," Erica said. "But I suppose I won't get you to change your mind." She looked into the mirror, where she could see Carol siting behind her. "How are you doing, Carol?"

"Good," Carol said. "Stressed about finals, but I'm sure it will be fine. I can't believe they're next week!"

"Neither can I," Erica said. "Another long year, over with. You'll do fine with your finals. Don't stress so much. They won't be as bad as you think. It's all in your head. Use a trick I used in college. If there are bonus questions, count them at the beginning. Whenever you get stressed, go and answer a bonus question to the best of your ability. It will relax you. Then continue with the exam. It won't guarantee you a good grade, but it will guarantee that you will finish the final without stress, which is more important in the long run."

"We're here," Lilly yelled.

Erica looked forward, and out the windshield. She found herself staring at the front doors of a strip club.

"Lilly," Erica said. "*Why on Earth* are we at a strip club?"

"Oh, come on," Lilly said." It'll be fun! I rented it out!"

"You did *what*," Erica exclaimed. "Who *rents out* a strip club?"

"It *is* a bachelorette party," Lilly replied.

"But there are only *three* of us," Erica yelled furiously. "Why would we need an entire strip club all to ourselves?"

"Look, I'm sorry," Lilly said. "I never would have done it if I knew you were going to make such a big deal out of it. Do you want me to go inside and cancel the reservation?"

"What for," Erica said. "We're already here, we might as well go inside."

"Okay, then let's go inside," Lilly said.

"Alright, let's go," Erica said, not moving a muscle.

"Okay," Lilly said. "After you, bride to be."

Erica opened the door, half angry, half excited, and stepped out of the car. Lilly got out next, and Carol got out third, looking nervously at the building. She hadn't had the slightest idea where they were going when they had picked her up at her house. All that she had been told was that it was Erica's bachelorette party and that Erica wanted her there.

When they walked in, they noticed first that the lighting was pretty dim. Erica pondered whether or not this was the same strip club that Robert had taken William to for his bachelor party. She figured that it must be, because she couldn't imagine that there were that many strip clubs in the near vicinity of where they lived.

"Hello ladies," said the man who was at the bar. "We've set up three seats and a small table right in front of the stage. I'll be over in a minute to take your drink orders."

They walked over to the seats and sat down.

"Lilly," Erica said inquisitively. "I'm not complaining, but we're at a strip club, so, where are the strippers?"

"Strippers," Lilly said with an evil grin. "What do you think I am, some kind of pervert?"

The entire room fell dark and within moments, the lights on the stage came on and three young, muscular men, who were only wearing thongs, were standing there. A techno song began blasting out of the speakers and the men began their dance routine.

Carol was embarrassed as she'd ever been in her life. She attempted to focus her attention on their carefully synchronized dancing, and tried to tell herself how much she loved the dancing technique. She tried, but then the dancers came off of the stage.

Each girl had a guy giving her a lap dance. Their muscles were reminiscent of a man in a magazine.

Carol began to experience something that she had not felt since she had bee with David. It was quite embarrassing, considering that her teacher was sitting in the next seat over. But after about half a minute, she relaxed, sitting back in her seat. She figured that it wasn't going away, so she might as well just enjoy the feeling while she had it.

The men were quite literally riding the girls. They stood up and thrust their pelvis' in their faces. The routine lasted about ten minutes in total and then they walked back onto the stage and then backstage.

"Still having second thoughts," Lilly asked Erica.

"Nope," Erica said, breathing heavily. She wiped some sweat from her brow. "Not at all."

"How are you holding up, Carol," asked Lilly.

Carol did not answer her, though. Her eyes were closed and she had a look on her face like she was *really* enjoying herself. She was breathing calmly and the smiling kept coming.

Erica and Lilly looked at each other and burst into a quiet laughter, not believing what they were witnessing.

"Okay," yelled the bartender, breaking the laughter, as well as breaking Carol out of her trance like state. "That was our opener. Who wants drinks?"

"The lucky lady and I will each have a beer," said Lilly. "Carol will have a glass of margarita mix."

"Mix," said the bartender, confused.

"She's under twenty-one," Lilly explained.

"Oh," said the bartender. "Usually people just hand us some bogus fake ID."

Erica chuckled, thinking of Robert. She didn't laugh too hard though, because as ridiculous as it was, it had worked.

The bartender brought over their drinks and set them on the table. They all picked their drinks up and took a sip.

"To the beginning of the rest of your life," Lilly said, holding up her glass. "Cheers."

Erica and Carol held their glasses up as well. They all clinked their glasses and then took another sip.

"Lilly," the bartender said.

Lilly looked at the bartender and he nodded, as though he were signaling something.

"Erica," Lilly said. "I wanted to do something extra special for you, seeing as how you are not only my sister, but my best friend as well."

"Lilly, what did you do *now*," Erica asked.

"Well, you know," Lilly said. "With all of us getting dances, it takes the glory off of you."

One of the dancers came out onto stage and set a chair in the middle of it. He stepped off and extended his hand to Erica. Erica reluctantly took his hand and he led her onto the stage and over to the chair, where she sat down.

He walked backstage to get the others. They all walked out onto the stage, now seemingly all dressed and were all wearing cowboy hats.

A loud, fast paced country song started and all three men surrounded Erica. They began by walking around her like they were playing a perverse version of musical chairs. As they walked, they began to slowly lose pieces of clothing, playfully whipping Erica with them before throwing them away. The music did not stop, but one of the men did sit down, on Erica's lap. At that point, all three of the men were down to nothing but their cowboy hats, their thongs and their cowboy boots.

He laid back and wrapped his arm around her neck. The other men got on either side of her and began dancing in place, as sexually as they could.

Lilly and Carol just watched, laughing quietly. Even though they thought it was funny, they were both a bit jealous as well. After an elongated performance, the same man who had brought her onstage took her off and led her back to her seat. He nodded at her, winked, and hopped back up onto the stage and walked backstage.

"Oh, that was fun," Erica said, laughing so hard she had tears running down her cheeks. "What's next?"

"Honestly," Lilly said. "Nothing. I thought after a couple of dances, we could just enjoy an hour or two of just chatting."

"I actually really like that idea," Erica said, finally relaxing again and taking another sip of her beer."

"So how excited are you for the wedding," Lilly asked.

"I'm really excited," Erica said. "I thought that by this time I'd be nervous, but I'm not. I'm just really excited! I really can't wait to be Mrs. William Morrison."

"I'm happy for you," Lilly said. "I can't wait to be able to finally call him, officially I mean, my brother in law."

"I'm really happy for you too," Carol said. "You two are so happy together. You're the perfect couple."

"Thank you, Carol," Erica said. "Well, what do you say ladies, one more round of drinks?"

"One more," Lilly said.

They got one more round of drinks and talked more, about the wedding, about the baby who would be born a couple of months later, about the baby shower, which Lilly was already planning, and just about life in general. They discussed the past, the present and the future. They laughed and talked for about an hour and a half more, and then they decided to go.

Lilly and Erica dropped Carol off outside her house, and then Lilly took Erica home.

"Lilly," Erica said as she got out of the car. "Thank you very much, I had a great time."

"I'm glad," Lilly said. "I just wanted something simple and sweet, just like you."

"Thanks," Erica said, smiling again. "I'll call you tomorrow."

"Okay, I love you," Lilly said.

"I love you too," Erica hollered as she walked inside.

She walked to her bedroom, where William was already sleeping and got undressed. She laid down and fell into a quick sleep and dreamed about the night, the dancers and most importantly of all, the good time she'd had with Lilly and Carol.

The last day was hectic, to put a word to it. It was always like this, William recalled as he sat in his classroom, staring hard at the clock, anticipating the final bell as much as the students. And it wasn't even eight o'clock yet.

The room was buzzing with loud chatter. Students were loudly talking about how well, or awful they thought they had done on their final exams. Some were talking about the summer, the trips they planned with their familys. They were a happy bunch. The ones who weren't as happy were the ones who thought that it was absolutely the most unfair thing in the world that their parents were making them get a job so that they could start saving for college.

Hearing that struck a nerve with William, who knew all too well how important it was to save money for college while in high school. But, though the thought was aggravating, he didn't mind. He was just happy that the year was coming to a close.

He was able, somehow, to drown out the loud talking of the students and relax, thinking of his own summer plans, which included his wedding and the birth of his first child.

David sat at his desk, anxiously tapping his foot on the floor. This day made no sense. They were there, essentially, to have an extended lunch, which was in honor of the seniors. The lunch would start in less than three hours, and then everyone would be outside, eating burgers and hot dogs.

David figured that it was a good idea for the seniors, who may not see their friends after their graduation that evening, but for him, his only friend that he planned on hanging out with for any amount of time over the summer would be Tim, and he only lived across town. Momentarily, this thought made him chuckle, and he was lost again in the thought that he was, in about five hours, going to be on summer vacation.

His summer vacations were always special to him, because they gave him time to write, *a lot*. And as an added bonus, this summer would give him more time to hang out with Tim. They would be able to hang out *any day they wanted*, which was a fantastic thought. David smiled at that thought and closed his eyes, relaxing in his chair.

In Erica's classroom, things were about the same. Students were all talking, about pretty much the same subjects. Erica, like William, was staring at the clock. She sipped her coffee and looked out into her group of students. She spotted Carol, who she shot a short wave to.

Caorl stood up and walked over to her desk.

"Good morning," Carol said. "Are you excited that it's the last day?"

"*Very,*" Erica said, smiling. "Do you have any plans for the summer?"

"Sleep, lay on the couch, write, the usual," Carol said thoughtfully. "And going to your wedding, of course. I can't forget that."

"No, me either," Erica said, staring thoughtfully at the wall. "I'm so nervous and excited at the same time. It's funny, at all of the weddings I've ever been to, I've been so bored. They're so long and seem meaningless. But thinking about weddings in the perspective that I'm having my own makes it so much better. I think it's the first wedding I've ever actually looked forward to going to."

"Not to be rude," Carol said. "But I actually feel the same way about weddings."

"It's not rude," Erica said. "At least not in my book. A lot of people feel that way about weddings. We feel obligated to go, no matter how close to the people we are. Family is family, we figure, and so we end up going."

"You always have such a realistic way of saying even the most simple things," Carol said. "I admire that."

"Thank you," Erica said.

The bell rang and Carol rolled her eyes.

"I guess I'll go sit in my 'class'," she said. "I'll talk to you later."

"Bye," Erica said, chuckling.

She took a long sip of her coffee and waited for her own 'class' to begin. She was just going to throw on a movie. Even if they didn't get to finish it, she figured, she had nothing else to do. As far as she was concerned, the school year was over.

Lunch time came quick enough, even if it felt like eternity. All of the students, and the faculty members who hadn't left yet gathered out back of the school, where the parking lot had been turned into a dining area, where the usual cooks were now manning two good sized grills. They were cooking, as promised, hamburgers and hot dogs.

The students and faculty members made a long line and got paper plates. They awaited their turn to get their lunch. Lunch usually started at eleven, but on the last day of school, it was always moved to ten thirty to accommodate the extra people.

Within twenty minutes, everybody had their food and were either sitting down or standing around, eating while they talked with their friends.

David was following around Tim, who was socializing with everybody. Tim seemed to have a knack for making friends with people of all groups, so he had a few senior friends who he wanted to say goodbye for in case their summer jobs affected their ability to see each other over the summer.

Carol quickly ate her food and then went to her locker. She loaded up what was left inside of it into her backpack and she walked to the lobby of the school. She waved at the secretary and told her to have a good summer. With that, she walked out of the front door and began the happiest walk home of the year.

As she walked, she leaned back in forth, dancing as she walked to a happy song that was playing inside of her head.

It was unbelievable that this was actually happening. William and Erica got into the car and William started the engine. Tomorrow, they were going to be getting married. As a wedding present, William had decided to take Erica back to the restaurant where they had shared their first date.

It was the first time since that first date that William had taken Erica back to this restaurant, mostly because, because of its significance, he had decided to only bring her back here for a special occasion. He figured that the night before their wedding fit that bill.

William pulled the car into the driveway of Eastman's and they got out of the car, both smiling. They walked into Eastman's and were seated. It wasn't the same exact table that they had sat at on their first date, but that didn't matter. All that mattered was the fact that they were at the same restaurant where they had gone on their first date.

They held their menu's in their hands and began looking.

"Steak," William said, thoughtfully.

"Same here," Erica said.

"Wine," William asked.

"Yes," Erica said.

"Excuse me," William said, catching a waiter as he walked by. "May we have a bottle of white wine?"

"Yes, I'll bring that right to you sir," the waiter said, walking off.

"Remember how awkward we were," Erica said. "The first time we were her?"

"Yes," William said, smiling. "We've certainly come a long way."

He reached across the table and took her hand in his. As he had said, the waiter came right back with the wine and two glasses. He placed one glass in front of each of them and poured wine for them.

"Are you ready to order," asked the waiter.

"We're both going to have steak," William said.

"Okay," the waiter said. "How would you like it?"

"Medium well done," said William.

"Same," Erica said.

"Okay," said the waiter, taking both of their menu's. He walked away from the table and William and Erica each lifted their glasses and their eyes caught each others.

"To us," William said. "To our marriage. To our family." Erica smiled.

"To our students, David and Carol, and all that they have learned in just one year," Erica said. They clinked their glasses and each sipped. Then they laughed.

"Do you think they would have lasted if he hadn't cheated on her," William asked.

"Hell no," Erica said, nearly falling out of her chair from laughing so hard. She settled down and got serious. "They were both too insecure. It wasn't just him cheating, it was also the fact that they had lost their virginity to one another. That did their relationship in right there."

"That's how it is with young love," William said. "It seems like these days it only lasts about two percent of the time."

"That's being generous," Erica said. "But they're both happier now, which is really all that matters, in retrospect."

"Yes," William said. "Young, happy writers with long, hope filled lives ahead of them. I envy them. I miss being their age. But, if I were to travel back in a time machine and be their age again, I would miss you, miss this. I would have to wait all this time again just to get back here, and I'm certain that this is all that I would think about, day in and day out, is getting to that first night where I met you."

"It sounds really corny," Erica said. "But there was something in your eyes that night. I don't want to be ridiculous and say that I *knew* that we would end up together, but I had a feeling. And I'm really happy that the feeling was correct."

"Me too," William said. "Truth be told, I had that feeling as well. I just never told you before now."

"William," Erica said. "Take a minute and just clear your mind. Picture it, tomorrow, we're going to be married. I will be Mr. William Morrison. I can't express through any words how happy that makes me. And then, a couple of months later, we're going to be parents."

"Two months ago, the thought of the entire situation put together scared the hell out of me," William said. "But now, thinking about it, and knowing that tomorrow we're going to be married, I'm not scared at all. I'm ecstatic!"

Their steak got there and they each cut their steak into ten smaller pieces. They ate their dinner and drank their wine in silence. A few times, they each tried to say something, but their excitement literately froze them in their tracks.

And so they just smiled at one another as they finished their meal. William paid the bill and they walked out to the car, hand in hand, heads touching. William held the door for Erica as she got in, and shut it. Then he walked over to the driver's side and got in.

As they drove home, their conversation was minimal, mostly once again mentioning the excitement of the day to come. They both wanted to have sex that night, but decided to wait until the following night as means of keeping *some* traditions. Even though it would not be, by a long shot, the first time they would have sex, something just felt right about doing it on their wedding night and so they did.

They kissed each other 'goodnight' and laid down. It was surprising how quickly they fell asleep. Later, they would figure that it must have been all the excitement that they had felt that day. It would be nice to say that their dreams had been about the day to come, but the fact was that *because* of the day to come, they slept so soundly that they did not remember any of their dreams in the morning.

CHAPTER 16

Over the last two weeks of school, Carol had become increasingly closer to Eliot, a fellow student who she had met in her English class. They had been friends in school for the succession of the class, but never outside of class. One day, out of the blue, Eliot asked Carol out, to which she said 'yes'. They had gone out that following weekend, to a local fast food restaurant. Eliot had apologized for the location, but had explained that he did not have a lot of money. Carol said that she understood and not to worry about it.

They had been dating ever since he had asked her out, hanging out at each others' houses and taking walks after school. They both hoped that they would be able to continue to stay close over the summer.

On the morning of the wedding, Erica was a blubbering mess. She hadn't anticipated that the actual day would be so overwhelming. Both her and William's mothers were trying their hardest to keep the makeup, which they were convinced she needed to wear, on even though her tears kept messing it up.

"I'm so sorry about the tears," Erica managed to say. "I'm just so happy!"

"It's fine, dear," said Mona. "We've all been through the same thing. We understand."

She couldn't bring herself to let go of her beautiful, white dress. It was the most beautiful thing she had ever seen. Through her tears, her smile was a big and bright as ever. Her jaws were killing her from the amount of smiling she was doing, but she didn't mind. Her happiness of the day would trump any pain that she felt.

"You're going to be fine," Robert said, patting William on his back.

"I know," William said. "Thanks. I'm just so nervous. I've never felt like this in my life."

"Once you're out there, you just have to stand there, remember that," Robert said. "All you have to remember is 'I do'. That's your only line. If you forget that, *then* you'll have a problem. And on top of all that, I'll be standing next to you the whole time."

"Thanks again," William said. "You're the best friend, and best man anyone could hope for."

"Don't you think it's a bit weird that you're going to a teacher's wedding," Tim asked over the phone. "*And* don't you think it's even *weirder* that you're going with your ex girlfriend *and* her boyfriend?"

"First off, Mr. Morrison is a major influence in my life, which is why I'm going," David responded. "And second, Carol's the only person I know who's going. Brenda will be working, so she won't be able to give me a ride."

"Alright, man," Tim said. "Call me whenever you get back, hopefully it's not that late. Maybe we can go to the movie's tonight."

"Sounds good," David said. "I've go to go anyway, I just heard a car pull into the driveway. Bye."

David hung up the phone and walked to the front door and looked out. Sure enough, there was Alice's car. He opened the door and walked out. He gave them each a small wave and then got into the backseat of the car.

"Hello," David said, nervously. He had no idea what reaction Alice would have to him riding in her car, nevertheless Carol's boyfriend.

"Hello, David," Alice said.

As he had hoped, Carol and Eliot didn't say anything. Alice tried to make small talk while they drove. Luckily, Erica's parents' house, where they were having the wedding in the backyard, was only a ten minute drive.

"How did you do on your final exams," Alice asked, hardly any care in her voice.

"Well enough," David said.

Alice nodded, and continued driving. She didn't speak one more word for the whole ride. In fact, she turned up the radio slightly to indicate, to David, that the conversation was over.

David was really nervous. He didn't know, when he got there, whether he should sit with them, since they were generous enough to give him a ride, or if he should sit somewhere else to avoid the awkwardness it would cause. He thought hard and finally agreed that he would sit in the opposite row. That didn't seem too rude, but it would keep them from having to speak to one another while they waited as well.

Finally, after what felt like an hour, they pulled into Erica's parents' driveway and parked. They silently got out of the car and walked out back, where guests were already sitting. David trailed behind to let Alice, Carol and Eliot sit down first. Once they did, he did as he planned and sat on the opposite row.

As he waited, he thought about the ending to a story that he would hopefully complete within the next couple of days. Suddenly, a girl walked up next to David.

"Do you mind if I sit here," she asked, pointing to the seat next to David.

"Not at all," David said, motioning her to the seat.

"Thank you," the girl said. She sat down and extended her hand. "My name's Lacy, I'm Erica's niece."

Lacy had long, dark brown hair, and dark brown eyes to match. She was wearing a beautiful red dress. When she sat down, David couldn't help but notice that she was also wearing perfume that smelled as pretty as she was.

"Hello," David said, shaking Lacy's hand. "I'm David, a student of William and Erica's."

"Cool," Lacy said. "Aunt Erica told me that a couple of her students were going to be here, but it was more in passing, so she didn't really say much about you."

The ceremony began and Lacy stopped talking, but the way she smiled at David told him that this short conversation would not be the last that he would share with her.

As Pachabel's "Canon" began, the wedding party began to come down the aisle. As they walked, cameras were flashing, people were quietly chatting among each other and every member of the wedding party held a very large smile on their face.

It was visible that Erica had been crying, but her smiles showed that they had been tears of joy, and so they brought even more smiles, not frowns, to the family and friends of her and William. They lined up, and the minister from Erica's parents' church took a step forward.

"We are gathered here today," the minister said. "To join these two people in holy matrimony."

The ceremony itself only took a few minutes, and pretty soon, it was the moment of truth.

"Do you, William Morrison, take this woman, Erica Young, to be your lawful wedded wife?"

"I do," William said.

"And do you, Erica Young, take William Morrison, to be your lawful wedded husband?"

"I do," Erica said.

"In that case," said the Minister, "I now pronounce you man and wife. William, you may kiss the bride."

William leaned in for the most passionate, emotional kiss he had, and ever would, share with anyone.

"Ladies and gentlemen," announced the Minister. "I give you, for the first time, Mr. and Mrs. William Morrison!"

Everyone stood up, cheered and applauded.

After the wedding party had departed, everyone rearranged the chairs and brought in tables from Erica's parents' basement and set them up for the reception.

Setting up took half an hour and then, when they were ready, Erica's mother went inside and told the wedding party that it was time to make their ways to the table at the head of the reception. They did so, and got another loud applaud as they did.

Everyone got themselves a plate and picked out a seat. David and Lacy sat down next to each other and David looked over at Lacy.

"I don't mean to be straightforward," David said. "Because I know what that can lead to. But you're beautiful."

"Well thank you," Lacy said. "You're pretty cute yourself."

"Thanks," David said, beginning to blush slightly.

"Nice wedding," Lacy said after a slight pause.

"Yeah," David said. "I liked that they had it at her parents' place. It gave it character."

"Character," Lacy asked.

"Yeah," David said. "Personality. I just mean that it was kind of an original idea. It wasn't just a church wedding. I've been to a couple of weddings for people who weren't even very religious, but they had their weddings in churches because they said it felt 'traditional'."

"I see your point," Lacy said. "I think it would be nice to have a beach wedding."

"Yeah," David said. "That would be beautiful."

David looked at Lacy when he said "beautiful". He smiled and looked away.

"I like you, David," Lacy said. "You're a good guy. Nicer than other guys I've met."

"Yeah, girls tell me that all the time," David said, sitting up and jokingly trying to look macho. Lacy laughed. "I'll bet."

"Do you want to go to the movies this weekend," David asked. "Just as friends, I mean that."

"Yeah," Lacy said. "I'd really like that. But only if you promise that you mean just as friends."

"I do," David said, smirking to himself at the irony of where he had just said that.

"Okay, then it's a yes," Lacy said. "I hate those people who jump right into relationships. It's so stupid."

"Yes it is," David agreed, looking down at the table.

"Look, they're cutting the cake," Lacy exclaimed.

David looked up and saw William and Erica, standing tall, both holding a knife. They brought the knife down on the cake and with two cuts, sliced out the first piece. Then they cut one more. They each picked one up and, as another tradition stands, smashed their pieces into each others faces. Everyone laughed and then some got in line to get their own cake.

"William," Erica said when they both sat back down at the table. "This is the happiest day of my life."

"You say that now," William said, pointing at her belly. "Wait until he, or she, is born."

"Okay, you win," Erica said. "Can you believe that we're married?"

"I know," William said. "It feels like a dream. And it's the happiest dream I've ever had."

William leaned in and kissed Erica. He embraced her, and they shared a long, loving kiss.

"Is it the wedding night," Erica said as she pulled her lips away from his.

"Almost," William said. "Eager, are we?"

"Maybe a little," Erica said, smiling. She leaned back in and kissed him again.

Without warning, Eliot walked up to David and took a deep breath.

"Hey, this is awkward, but neither one of them wanted to speak to you," Eliot said. "So they sent me over to tell you that we're going to be heading out in a couple of minutes."

"Oh, that's okay," Lacy said. "My mom will drop you off at your house."

"Are you sure," David asked.

"Pretty sure," Lacy said, smiling.

"Okay," David said. "Tell Alice I said 'thank you' for the ride."

"Alright," Eliot said, turning. "See you around."

Lacy's mother, Anna, said 'yes', just as Lacy had said she would and they left at six thirty, after saying goodbye to William and Erica. They walked to the parking lot and found Anna's car. David wanted nothing more than to slip his hand into Lacy's, but if his long, bumpy Freshman year had taught him, it was that too forward led to too many problems.

Lacy sat in the front seat, next to Anna, but she was turned around so that she could see David. After David told Anna where he lived, they were off.

"So what do you like to do," Lacy asked.

"I enjoy writing," David said, half expecting her to tell him that it was a silly thing to do.

"Me too," Lacy exclaimed.

"Really," David said. "That's awesome! What do you write?"

"Some mystery," Lacy said. "But mostly horror. You?"

"Horror," David responded, grinning from ear to ear.

"Great," Lacy said. "It looks like we'll have a lot to talk about."

"Yeah, it does," David said.

They got to David's house and he said thank you to Anna and got out of the car. Lacy got out too. She handed David a napkin with her number on it.

"Call me Thursday and we'll set up a time and place to meet to go to the movie," Lacy said.

"Great," David said. "I will."

"Talk to you soon," Lacy said.

"Yes," David said. "I'll talk to you soon too."

Lacy gave him a quick wave as she got into the car. David waved back and then turned. He began walking toward the house, disbelieving the fact that he had met Lacy, completely by chance, and made a new friend. He went inside and grabbed the phone. He had to tell Tim about Lacy.

Tim was really happy for David and he really wanted to meet Lacy. He told David that they should get all get together to go to the movies.

"That's actually a fantastic idea," David said. "Neither of us wanted it to be a date, so if I bring a friend, it won't be. Just some friends hanging out."

"Alright," Tim said. "Call me back after you set it up."

David called Lacy as soon as he hung up the phone and set up the time and place to meet on Friday evening. He told her that Tim wanted to go so that he could meet her, and she said that was cool, so he called Tim back and told him.

"Alright," Tim said. "So we'll all meet there around six thirty?"

"That's the plan," David said. "See you then."

Friday came and David couldn't sit still all day. He tried to write to take his mind off of the excitement, but it didn't work. He paced around his room all day, singing and dancing as well. He was doing anything he could think of to make the time pass.

Finally, it was six o'clock, and he practically ran out the door. He jogged the entire way to the movie theater, and when he got there, he felt silly because neither Tim or Lacy were there yet. He stood outside of the movie theater, where they had said they would meet, and waited, impatiently.

Tim showed up five minutes later and danced up to him.

"So, where is she," Tim asked, smiling like a madman.

"She's not here yet," David said with a chuckle. "But she should be here anytime now."

Just as said that, Anna's car appeared in front of them and parked. Lacy got out and said goodbye to Anna.

"Hey," Lacy exclaimed. She ran up to David and gave him a hug.

"Hey," David said, hugging her back. "This is Tim."

Tim said 'hi' and reached out his hand. They shook hands and then David looked at the door.

"Are you guys ready to head in?" Tim asked.

They both nodded and David opened up the door, leading them both in with his hands. David walked in and they all got into line.

They got their tickets, as well as a small popcorn each, and a Pepsi. They walked into the theater and took three seats in the back row. They were the most excited three individuals in the crowd, or at least that's what they figured.

"This is going to be so fun," David said.

"Yeah," Lacy said. "It's so rare that a good horror film is actually released into theaters these days. And I hear this one is *fantastic*!"

"I've heard really good things about it too," David said.

"It's only been out for a week and it already has a 7.9 on IMDB," Tim said. "That's pretty good for a horror film."

"Definitely," Lacy agreed.

"Hey, look," David said, pointing down to the front row. "It's William and Erica."

"This is our first official date as a married couple," William said. "I just realized that."

"I know," Erica said. "It's really nice. The funny thing is that it doesn't feel like anything's changed."

"I know," William said. "Everyone says marriage changes everything."

"I thought that was sex," Erica said.

"I think it's both," William said.

"Maybe," Erica said. "But I agree, I haven't seen any real changes yet. Can I have some popcorn?"

Carol and Eliot got to the theater later than they had planned, but they were still on time, so they weren't complaining. They got their tickets, some popcorn and Pepsi's and walked inside to the theater. They took two end seats, near the middle, and got comfortable.

"I really like you, Carol," Eliot said.

"I really like you too Eliot," Carol said. "But I told you already, we're going to take this slow. I've been down that fast track road before and it's not fun, believe me. I know it sounds fun, jumping right in bed with one another and such, but it only leads to problems. Then we'll probably end up breaking up, and I don't want that, because you're one of the nicest guys I've ever met."

The lights went down and all of the chatter that had been going on throughout the theater quieted down. William had his arm around Erica, who had her head comfortably on his shoulder.

David, Lacy and Tim sat, side by side, unconsciously putting popcorn into their mouths, ready for anything. Carol held Eliot's hand in hers, lightly. They sat silent, staring at the movie screen, occasionally eating a piece of popcorn.

It had been a long Freshman year, filled with events which ranged from really awesome to really awful. It was a year in a high school. William and Erica had both found true love, an idea which they both would have laughed at on that first day of the school year. David and Carol had fallen in and out of love, which was one of the greatest experiences that they had ever had. They now knew a lot more about romance, and they were both on the fast track to success in that area.

David had Lacy, Carol had Eliot, and both couples had agreed to take it slow. Whether they stuck to that agreement or not was another thing, but they would have to cross that bridge when they got to it. Right now, everyone was content, even Tim, whose only true love was his writing.

They could only wonder if their Sophomore year would have as many twists and turns as their Freshman year had. Assumption, as well as high school TV dramas, told them that it would, and that was fine. They had learned a lot over the year, but most importantly, they had learned that life has ups and downs. It's funny, in more ways than one. Life isn't always what you want it to be, but as they had all discovered, that's life.

ABOUT THE AUTHOR

Kenneth Winfield Emerton has lived in Maine his entire life. He has been writing since second grade. His hometown is Blue Hill, but he moved to Bucksport at the age of eight. In 2007, he began his freshman year at Bucksport High School, which became a part of the inspiration for his first book, "Freshman Year."

Printed in the United States
By Bookmasters